Oy, Joy!

Oy, Joy!

a novel by

Lucy Frank

Aladdin Paperbacks
New York London Toronto Sydney Singapore

First Aladdin Paperbacks edition July 2001

Aladdin Paperbacks
An imprint of Simon & Schuster
Children's Publishing Division
1230 Avenue of the Americas
New York, NY 10020

The text for this book was set in 11-point Stempel Garamond.

Printed and bound in the United States of America

10 9 8 7 6 5 4 3 2 1

The Library of Congress has cataloged the hardcover edition as:

Frank, Lucy.
Oy, Joy! / Lucy Frank.
p.   cm.
Summary: Although her ailing uncle creates problems for her whole family when he moves in with them, Joy survives his bungling attempts at matchmaking even as she plays the game herself.

ISBN: 0-7894-2538-6 (hc.)
[1. Uncles—Fiction. 2. Family life—Fiction. 3. Friendship—Fiction. 4. Interpersonal relations—Fiction.] I. Title.
PZ7.F85150y 1999 [Fic]—dc21 98-54299 CIP AC
ISBN: 0-689-84318-6 (Aladdin pbk.)

For Marion and Irwin Kaplan

And to the memory of my father, who never stopped believing he was Uncle Max.

Chapter 1

"Joy, you're not concentrating," said my friend Maple. We'd just gotten through the first three days of high school. Now we were sprawled on my bedroom rug filling out a Match Quiz. Or rather, Maple was. I'd spent the past half-hour decorating the form with little kangaroos. " *'What do people think is my best quality?*

1. *Intelligence*
2. *Personality*
3. *Honesty*
4. *Looks*
5. *Enthusiasm*
6. *Apartment without parents.*' "

"This quiz should come with a manual," I said.

"Exactly," she said. "Do I put down who *I* am or who *they* are, or who I want people to *think* I am? I mean, are we doing this to attract people I *should* meet, or the kind of people I'd really like?"

"No clue," I said, giving one kangaroo a pair of shoes.

"Well, what'd you put for number two?" she said. " 'The first word most people think of when they think of me is . . .

> 1. Hot
> 2. Cool
> 3. Funny
> 4. Interesting
> 5. Depressing
> 6. Boring
> 7. Dead.' "

"I don't know. These are all either too normal or too negative," I said. "Where're bizarre, bonkers, berserk, bats, bananas—"

"What if people don't think of me at all?" Maple said. "What if none of these choices fit? Does that make me a Match Quiz misfit? Does it mean they won't find matches for me?"

The great thing about having a best friend is how you can take turns being anxious. "Maple," I said. "You're making this into way too big a deal. You're acting like this is our only chance to meet people."

"Not people," she said. "Boys. There are sixteen hundred kids in this school, remember? We've met what, thirty of them, twenty-nine of them girls? We could be juniors before we have a social life."

"Come on," I said, "how serious can you get about questions like *'Your ideal date is:*

>   *1. Dinner and a movie*
>   *2. Bungee jumping*
>   *3. Rock concert*
>   *4. I prefer not to meet in person.'* "

"Yeah, well," she said, "I've heard a lot of people talking, and they say it works. Boys really call and ask you out. Or you call them. Or meet them, whatever. . . ."

It wasn't that I didn't want to meet a boy. I thought about it every time I saw a couple who really liked each other. "Fine," I said. "Let's do it." I picked up the sheet and read: " *'Which of these words most closely describes your hair?*

>   *1. Blond*
>   *2. Brown*
>   *3. Black*
>   *4. Lime green*
>   *5. Gray*
>   *6. I have no hair to speak of.'* "

"I guess black," she said.

"Put lime," I said. Her hair was all black now, but

last week only one side was black and the month before it was purplish pink. "It might be by the time they score this. What would you call mine?"

"Brown," she said.

"Brown's so blah," I said. "It's so generic. I wish I could put chestnut, or honey, or honey nut." She rolled her eyes. I checked number two, Brown. " '*My favorite outfits come from . . .*

1. *Great-Aunt Minnie*
2. *Prep Town*
3. *The land of dead jeans*
4. *The mall*
5. *Bloomingdale's.*' "

I supposed my ravel-hemmed jeans and T-shirt—the same jeans and T-shirt as ninety percent of the teenage girls in New York City, if not the universe—made me a number three, but I drew in a sixth box: "Other." Maple loved having people notice her, which is why she had on seven earrings, an orange lace top, overall shorts with fishnet stockings, and one red sneaker and one blue sneaker.

" '*Do you have an imaginary friend?*' " she read.

" '*1. No*
2. *His name is Roy and I resent your calling him imaginary.*' "

"One! No!" I said. In fact, her name was Kestrel and she was a bird girl, though I wasn't sure if she still counted as an imaginary friend, or just a character I drew. Not even Maple had seen my Kestrel notebooks.

The door opened. "Can you help me catch Kurt Cobain?" asked my brother.

"Close the door!" cried Maple. "We don't want rodents running in here!"

"Kurt doesn't like being called a rodent," said Nathan. "But don't worry. He's under my dresser. Ludwig's still in the cage."

"Why'd you open it?" I asked. This happened at least once a week. He'd had the mice since last year's science project, when he'd played Kurt a Nine Inch Nails tape twelve hours a day and locked Ludwig in the closet with nonstop Mozart, to see if it affected their personalities. Clearly it had.

"It smelled," he said, jingling the change in his pocket. Nathan's always fiddling or twiddling with something. "I was going to clean it. Come on, Joy. It will only take a minute."

"Get Mom to help this time," I said. My mother actually thought the mice were cute. But then, she thought Nathan was cute.

"She's not home yet," he said. "She's stopping at the hospital again to see Uncle Max. Come on, please? I'll catch him. You just have to move the dresser." He picked up my Match Quiz. " '*When kissing,*' " he read, before I could grab it away, " '*do you keep your eyes . . .*

    1. Open
    2. Closed
    3. On your wallet.'

What *is* this?"

"It's a Match Quiz," said Maple. "For freshmen to meet people. For two dollars, you get the names and numbers of the twenty people whose answers most closely match your own. They'll match us up with kids from the whole school or just our grade. It's like a fund-raiser, to help pay for school dances, stuff like that."

" '*How do you usually find a date?*' " he read in what he clearly meant to be a TV game-show-host imitation.

    " '*1. I ask everyone I meet*
    2. I continually call them for the homework, even if they're not in my grade
    3. I wait for him/her to ask me
    4. I'm relying on this quiz.'

Uh, Joy?" He raised an eyebrow. "You've never even had a date."

This was a piece of information I did not need to hear out loud. But Maple jumped in and said, so matter-of-factly that I could have kissed her, "That's right. That's why we're doing this."

"Yeah," he said, "but the questions are so stupid."

"If I help catch Kurt," I asked him, "will you leave?" He nodded. "Promise?"

We went in and moved his dresser. Kurt, as usual, was cowering under it. Nathan grabbed him and plopped him in the cage with Ludwig. Then I went back to my room and shut the door. Maple had moved onto my bed. I sat down next to her and looked at the questions for what must have been the fifteenth time:

Your lifestyle can best be described as:

> 1. *Alternative*
> 2. *Mainstream*
> 3. *Life? What life?*

If you were an ice-cream flavor, would you be:

> 1. *Chocolate*
> 2. *Vanilla*
> 3. *Chunky monkey*
> 4. *Rocky road.*

"Nathan's right," I said. "These are stupid questions."

"Come on. Just do your best," Maple said.

"I am," I said, looking at my answers. "But I mean, vanilla ice cream, brown hair, dead jeans, no life? That's not me."

"You could change your image," she said.

"I could change the questions. I mean, even *'What's your favorite color?'* would tell you more than these do." I loved every bright color—tulip red, parrot green, dandelion yellow—even if I didn't wear them.

I'd begun drawing a little guy in a hat climbing out of a kangaroo's pouch, but I could see Maple was losing patience with me, so I went back to putting X's in the little boxes. I was still grappling with what grade-level date I preferred when Mom knocked.

"Maple's staying, okay?" I said, quickly turning over my Match Quiz.

"Not tonight, Joy." Mom looked tense and worried.

"Why? What's up?" I asked.

She didn't answer me. "I'm sorry, Maple," she said. "The family has something serious to discuss. We need to have a family meeting."

"It's about Uncle Max," she said once Maple had gone and we were all seated at the table. "Joy, are you listening?"

"Sorry," I said. I began thinking up my own match questions. *If you were a mountain, would you be:*

1. *Mount Rushmore*
2. *Mount Everest*
3. *Mount Vesuvius*
4. *A molehill.*

If you were a lower life form, would you be:

1. *A coral snake*
2. *A toadstool*
3. *A butterfly*
4. *A chameleon*
5. *A Venus flytrap*
6. *An acorn squash.*

"We're going to need everyone's cooperation," Mom said. "They're letting Uncle Max out Monday, and we don't see how he can possibly go back to the apartment. I've talked with Social Services, and I stopped over today to check on the poor dog. That nice lady next door, Mrs. Nussbaum, is still walking him. She told me this wasn't Uncle Max's first episode. He's blacked out and fallen a few times and never said anything. He can't live alone! The social worker suggested some sort of aide, but can you see him putting up with that? He never even wanted a cleaning lady."

"He'd fire her the first day," Dad said. "If she didn't jump out the window first."

"Marty! He's not that bad." She gave Dad a warning look.

"So what are you saying?" I asked.

"We don't have another choice," she said. "He's going to have to move in with us."

"For how long?" Nathan asked.

"Just till we can get him situated properly," Dad said. Mom frowned. "Ilene," he said in a way that let me know they'd been over this a lot, "there has to be some sort of comfortable senior housing—"

"What about Sarge?" I asked.

"Oh, Lord!" Dad rolled his eyes. I could see his point. Sarge wasn't the world's most attractive dog.

Mom's lips tightened. "We wouldn't even have this place if it weren't for Uncle Max."

"I know," Dad said. He looked even more stressed out than he usually did after work. "You don't have to keep reminding me. Besides, we've almost paid him back."

"We are not putting my uncle in some nursing home," she said. "It isn't right. That's not how you take care of family. You know what he did for me when Mother died, and let's not forget the years you worked for him. . . ."

"Believe me, I have not forgotten them," Dad said.

I looked around our cluttered living room, which

already served as living room and dining room, not to mention my mother's office. "Where's he going to stay?" I said. "There's no room for him."

"He's going to need a real bedroom," Mom said. "You and Nathan will have to double up."

Chapter 2

I didn't see how this could work. Uncle Max's personality aside, I couldn't imagine having a sick eighty-year-old man in our apartment, even if he was practically our closest relative. Uncle Max was Mom's uncle, my great-uncle. Back when Dad was still hoping that someday he'd be able to make a living as an artist, he'd worked for Uncle Max and Uncle Nathan at Nathan's Shoes, the store where every kid on the Upper West Side gets his Keds. Uncle Max took us out for pastrami sandwiches the first Sunday of every month. He still sent me valentines signed "Your Secret Pal," and every week mailed us an envelope full of financial tips and editorials and health columns he'd cut out from *The New York Times*. But Mom was taking two night courses this semester, as well as teaching full-time. Dad was putting in long hours at the office. Nathan was eleven. That left only me to take care of him. I'd seen him just once since his stroke, the day after it happened.

He'd looked so small and helpless lying in that hospital bed, with a bandage on his head and a tube taped in his nose. Mom promised he was nothing like that now. But this sounded scary.

Also, Nathan wasn't terrible, as little brothers go, but share a room with him?

"Why can't you just sleep in the living room?" Maple asked me on the phone that night. "Or Nathan can. You'll take his room."

"Where would Mom work?" I asked. "She does homework every night, plus grading papers."

"Couldn't she work in the kitchen or move her desk into her bedroom?"

"There's no room," I said. "Dad's got all his painting stuff in there."

"Well, maybe your uncle will refuse," she said. "He's used to living by himself. I think there's hope, Joy. Unless he's really losing it, he won't agree."

But he did, even though he'd started out saying he'd rather be put in a home than impose on us, because none of the places Dad called allowed animals.

He was getting out on Monday. Friday night, Mom and Dad brought Sarge back with his bag of dog chow and his leash and his brush and his medications. Sarge is an elderly, overweight terrier with one of those lampshadelike cones around his head to keep him from scratching all his skin off. I'd always figured he was named after Sargent's flea collars. Dad said it wasn't fleas; it was a nervous condition. Sarge did seem very tense. He barked every time the elevator stopped at our floor. "I'm sure he'll relax," Mom said.

"Why? Max never has," Dad said.

Dad flat out didn't like Sarge. Nathan ignored him. Mom took him on, the way she did everything else. I felt sorry for him. "It's okay, boy," I kept telling him, as he ran from one room to the other, sniffing all the corners. I'd never realized a dog could look so worried. "I know you're looking for Uncle Max. He'll be here soon."

My parents decided Uncle Max would take my room because it was closer to the bathroom. "It's not as if we're asking you to sleep on Nathan's top bunk," Mom said. "We'll partition the room. You'll still have your own room, in effect, just smaller. We can even paint your side a different color."

"Black," I said.

"Not black." Sarcasm goes right by Mom. "Something pretty and cheerful. We'll get you some new curtains, too, and a new bedspread, maybe a new rug. Come on. Let's measure everything. We'll get some bookcases at one of those unpainted furniture places on Broadway and use them as a divider. I think we can make this work."

Since it seemed to be happening, like it or not, I

hoped she was right. And bookcases actually sounded like a good idea. So Saturday morning, we went out and bought the four tallest, heaviest ones we could find, and when they arrived, we pushed all my brother's furniture to what was now his side. Poor Sarge got stepped on a few times, but we eventually got the bookcases lined up down the middle of the room. Then Mom and Dad helped carry in all my books and clothes. They moved my posters for me and my radio and my CDs, but I said I'd deal with the personal stuff.

The main thing was my Kestrel notebooks. I had to find a place for them where Nathan, who was well known for poking around in people's things, wouldn't think to look. In the top of my closet, I found an old My Little Pony laundry bag. Even Nathan couldn't think that was interesting. I tucked the notebooks in it and stashed it in the bottom dresser drawer. Then we moved my furniture to Nathan's room—all but my desk and the bottom half of my high-riser bed, which we left for Uncle Max.

"Boy, are we lucky to have such big rooms," Mom said.

I didn't say anything. I hadn't realized the bookcases would take up so much space. My side felt more like a corridor than a bedroom.

"Don't get upset yet," Mom said. "We're not finished."

Dad pushed Nathan's desk a little farther from his drum set. "Lots of kids have rooms smaller than this," he said. "I think my room, growing up, was smaller. Look, Joy." He shoved my chest of drawers across the entrance to my side. "This'll give you a lot more privacy." It did make a partial barricade, but Nathan could still walk in at any time.

"Well, at least you'll finally have enough room for all your books," Mom said. "And you each still have a nice big window." But the bookcases were two feet lower than the ceiling and four feet shorter than the room. I'd see Nathan if he was going toward the door or was over at the closet, which we now had to share. And there was another problem. There was no place for my desk.

"Where do we put the computer?" I asked.

Mom looked at Dad. Her smile was starting to look kind of strained. "We'll figure something out," he said.

"Like what?" I said. "Do my homework in the closet?"

His eyes brightened. "Joy, that's a great idea! The cedar closet may actually be big enough." For someone so sarcastic himself, he sure wasn't picking up on mine. He got his tape measure, and we followed him to the foyer. He opened the door and pulled the light string. "Look. See how deep it is? If we take out all the boxes and the grocery cart, and move the ironing board and your bikes into our room, and bring in a power cord, it might just work. We can even find room for the printer."

"But now you have to put all that stuff in your room," I reminded them.

"I'm pretty sure we can hang the bicycles from the ceiling," he said.

"Yeah, we all have to flex," Mom said.

An hour later, my computer was up and running. "Joy, you're a genius!" she said. "Look at this, you solved it!" Yes, I wanted to say, but I meant it as a joke. "See, it's fine, if you don't push the chair back too far." She'd put an old piece of green carpeting on the floor, pinned a calendar on the wall, and squeezed a wastebasket in the corner. "It might be a little stuffy with the door closed, but the cedar fragrance will be great." She put her arm around me. "I'm proud of you. We're doing the right thing, you know. Really. That's what counts."

I thought how much easier it'd be to have an obnoxious mom, like Maple's, or a mean mom—someone you could yell and scream at, instead of always wanting to agree with her so that she'd stop looking so distressed. I went back to Nathan's room, hoping it wasn't as bad as I remembered. "Nathan?" I heard the Game Boy, but I didn't see him. "Nathan?" I looked in the closet. There was no sign of him. *Blip! Bleep!* I looked up. He was lying on top of the bookcases, with his blanket and pillow and a pile of comics.

"Like my new perch?" he said. "It's great. You can come up here, if you want."

"Thanks, but no thanks," I said.

"It won't fall over. I put my rock collection on the bottom shelves, plus the meteorite pieces. Plus I loaded it with books. You just climb the shelves like a ladder. Try it. Really. It's the best place in the house."

"For you, maybe." Why did Nathan's life seem so much simpler? Give him some little thing to fiddle-diddle with and he was happy. "Anyway, do you have to do that now?" I said. He stopped, but a minute later, started fiddling with the Snapple caps he always carries in his pockets, pressing them in and out, which made a clicking noise almost as irritating as the Game Boy. "Can you cut the clicking?" I said. He did, but then he began blowing his nose. Nathan never blows his nose just once. It's always like, "Honk! *Honk! HONK!*" like a goose having a conniption. Except at the moment it wasn't funny.

I took my pillow off the bed and went back to my room. It looked grungy and forlorn, big clumps of dust clinging to the walls where furniture had been. Usually when I'm upset, I lock my door and turn up the music and work on my notebooks. Now, though, I just turned off the light and lay down on what had become Uncle

Max's bed. From somewhere in the room, I heard the sound of scratching and a snuffling wheeze. Sarge had made himself a nest in some dropped clothes. He heaved himself up and waddled toward me. "You're in the wrong room, dog," I said. "You don't want to be with me. I'm depressed."

He didn't care. He jumped onto the bed, turned around three times, and settled himself against my side. "Great," I said. "Just move right in. Take the whole bed while you're at it. Make yourself at home." He leaned into me. I scratched his head. He wriggled closer. A wave of doggy odor wafted over me. "This isn't going to work, Sarge," I said. "You smell. And that lampshade thing is poking me." I shifted him. He nudged me with his nose. He kept on nudging till I realized he was asking to be scratched some more. I scratched till I got tired of it. He pawed my arm. I held his foot to make him stop, and he finally relaxed. "Oh, God, Sarge," I said, still hand-in-paw with him, curling myself around him as he settled in to sleep. "Look at us. We're pathetic. You're supposed to be out chasing mailmen, having a good time. I don't know what I'm supposed to be doing, but it sure isn't this!"

Chapter 3

Uncle Max started calling from the hospital at six A.M. Monday. "When are you getting here?" he said. "I've been ready for an hour." We'd been up almost that long, doing the final cleaning and rearranging, making room in closets, taping down the rugs so he wouldn't trip on them with his walker, getting stuff out of the medicine chest to make room for his pills. My parents had taken the day off to get him moved. "Don't let me forget to bring over Sarge's leather bones," he said. "We don't want him chewing up your furniture." That call came while I was stripping what was now his bed. The last few calls were during breakfast. "Did anyone remember to notify the seltzer man? Did you leave the change-of-address card for the mailman? Did you cancel my *New York Times*?"

By seven thirty, Dad, on his fifth cup of coffee, was bouncing off the walls, while Mom fretted over last-minute items Uncle Max might need. Nathan, fully dressed, his backpack on, was wandering around in his socks looking under things. "I know they're somewhere," he kept saying. "Are you sure you haven't seen them?" Then, once he'd found the sneakers: "Do you know where I put my hat?"

"Which hat?" Dad said, knowing full well Nathan meant his Joe Tucciarone Sports Camp hat, which he'd practically slept in since Mom sewed on the Most Improved Player patch he'd won last summer. "Now what?" Dad groaned, when the phone rang again.

It was Maple. "How soon can you be at the bus stop?" she said. She dropped her voice. "Bring earrings and makeup and anything else you can think of."

"What's up?" I said. "Are you okay?"

"Pictures," she said. "Don't tell me you forgot. School pictures today. And no, I'm not okay. Mom went berserk and hid everything—my makeup, my hair stuff, even my earrings. Wait till you see what she's made me wear. Bring your overalls."

"I'm wearing them," I said.

"Change, please, I'm desperate. She's guarding me. I brought the phone into the bathroom."

"I have to leave," I told Mom. I ran first to my jewelry box, then switched the overalls for jeans, grabbed what little makeup I owned, my Ultra Mega Hold hair spray, and all my clips, barrettes, and scrunchies. Then I went to my parents' bathroom, took Mom's Treasure Trove of Beauty—one of those eighty-color sets she'd bought once on an impulse and never used—stuffed it in my backpack with my lunch, binder, the overalls, and my twenty pounds of books. I grabbed my now-cold bagel and headed for the door.

"Good Lord, Maple!" I said when I saw her at the bus stop. "You look so . . . dignified. You look like a flight attendant. You could get a job at, like, American Airlines, or Budget Rent-a-Car. You could be a tour guide, giving guided tours of, like, the Washington Monument, or—"

"Hey!" she said. "I told you it was serious." Her hair was parted and hanging straight, her face was bare, and she was wearing a navy knee-length pleated skirt and a white short-sleeved blouse with a round collar. She glanced around. "I'll die if we see anyone we know. What'd you bring?" I pulled out the Treasure Trove. "Oh, thank you!" she said. "Joy, I love you! You're my savior." We opened it as soon as we were on the bus. It was full of the most gorgeous peacock colors, which is what I would have chosen if I were a makeup sort of person, but she stuck to the dark shades—dark blue around her eyes, black inside her eyelids, black mascara. "See," she said, "I look more like me already."

She pulled her top hair into a sprig, secured it with a scrunchie, and sprayed the ends so they stuck out like a pinwheel. "Mom acts like this is a normal thing to do, to, like, steal my stuff, to raid my personal belongings. . . . I mean, it's not like I'm mutilating myself." She outlined her lips in black eyeliner, then filled them in with burgundy. "It's not like I have a tongue ring or a tattoo. And who is she to tell me what my own face should look like? And make me dress like a fifty-five-year-old lady!" A fifty-five-year-old lady across the aisle glared at us. I poked Maple, who glared back at her. "And you know why she's doing this, right? So she can send pictures to New Jersey to show them what a wholesome influence she is and how I'm totally transformed now that I'm with her instead of Dad."

The doors hadn't quite opened when we got to school, so she studied my earring collection while we waited on the steps. But before she could pick anything, this roly-poly person we knew from junior high, Justin Zuwadski, came barreling up. He was wearing a tie, and his hair, which usually stuck up like Sarge's brush, was plastered down. "Hey," he said, braces gleaming. "Whatcha doing?" He plunked himself right next to us.

"Exactly what it looks like," I said as Maple chose a tree frog and a little dolphin and a seabird for her left ear. "Maple, maybe try that little lobster on the bottom."

"Is there some reason most of your earrings are birds or fish?" she said.

"Lobsters aren't fish," Justin said. He kept staring at me. "They're crustaceans. And dolphins are mammals. So d'you fill out that match thing?" He had a really loud, annoying voice.

William Chan, also from junior high and even roly-poly-er, came up behind Justin. "He's hoping he gets matched up with you." Was that because he thought I was roly-poly, too? I thought of another match question: *Bee is to honey as . . .*

> 1. *Nerd is to Joy*
> 2. *Joy is to fiasco*
> 3. *Joy is to exit*
> 4. *All of the above.*

I stood up, but William just wouldn't quit. "Don't wait for the Match Quiz, man. This looks like a match to me right here. Make it easy on everybody. Ask Joy out."

"What is it with me?" I asked Maple when we'd finally escaped. "Nerds are just drawn to me. Chubby nerds. I have this, like, chubby nerd magnetism."

"Right," she said, "and that's exactly why we did the Match Quiz. Come on, I have only a few minutes to get changed."

"I should never have put that ninth graders were okay," I said as we headed for the girls' room, "or that looks were a low priority." *What is important to me is:*

1. *Simplifying the tax code*
2. *Stopping teen smoking*
3. *Developing some social skills*
4. *Getting out of this alive.*

"They're going to match me up with Justin *and* William. I just know it." I pointed to a boy who looked like a very tall anteater. "You watch. I'll get *him,* too."

"Joy?" She turned to me. "You're not getting nervous about this match thing, by any chance?"

"No!" I said, a lot louder than I'd planned. Luckily, the girls' room was still empty. *My biggest fear is:*

1. *Global warming*
2. *Snakes*
3. *Math*
4. *Tidal waves*
5. *Soft-boiled eggs*
6. *Looking stupid*
7. *Embarrassing myself*
8. *Rejection.*

"How's this?" She turned her blouse around backward, rolled the sleeves, and turned up the collar, then put on my overalls. She stuck her tongue out at her reflection. "God, I wish I could be like you, Joy. You can just wear that old T-shirt and no makeup and not worry about it."

I looked at myself in the mirror. "Is that a compliment or an insult?"

"Compliment, you moron." She came over behind me and undid the clip holding back my hair, then mushed her fingers through it till the curls puffed out around my head. "See, that's all you need."

"Really?" I could never tell how I looked.

"Yeah, live dangerously."

"It's not too frizz-oid?"

"Frizz-oid is you," she said. "Trust me. Stop worrying. We might not even need the Match Quiz. For all you know, you're gonna walk right out this door and meet someone totally, unbelievably fantastic."

Chapter 4

"Oy!" said Uncle Max. He was in Dad's favorite chair, *The New York Times* draped over his walker, Sarge lying at his feet. "Ilene," he said to Mom, who was sitting at the table folding laundry. "Ilene, that's not Joy, is it?"

"Put on your glasses, Max," my mother said. "That's Joy's friend, Maple." She was speaking much louder than normal. "You've met Maple."

Maple, during the course of the day, had improved her outfit with a pink rhinestone starburst pin she'd found in her locker, changed her lips to lavender, and paved the front of her hair with all-different-colored barrettes. "Hello, Mr. Mitnick," she shouted. "Hi, Nathan." My brother was lying on the floor bleeping his Game Boy. "He doesn't look that bad," she whispered.

"Thank God!" I whispered back. Uncle Max was very pale, but his blue eyes were as bright as they'd always been. And in his brown suit and yellow sleeveless sweater, which he wore no matter what the season, and his shiny black shoes, and his thin, white hair neatly brushed, if it weren't for the walker, you wouldn't have known he'd had a stroke. "How are you, Uncle Max?" I yelled, too. "You look okay," I shouted. "You look really great."

"He still needs to take it easy," Mom said.

"Not that easy," he said. His voice always sounded like he'd just smoked ten cigars. "But you don't need to shout. The ears work fine. It's the legs that don't work so good. Though I don't think I'll need this walker in a day or two." He looked at Maple. "It's not Halloween already, is it? You look like you're all set for trick or treat."

"The kids dress this way these days, Max," my mother said.

"Not me," Nathan said.

"I was being sarcastic, Ilene," Uncle Max said. I gave Maple a look. "I know how the kids dress. I see them every day." He motioned to me. "So, Miss High School Girl, come over and give your old uncle a kiss. I'd come to you, but it'd take me an hour to get up."

I went over and leaned down. He smelled, as always, like Old Spice. Dear God, I prayed, don't let him pinch my cheek.

"How'd you get so grown-up?" he said after he'd

released my face. He looked at my sneakers. "What are you up to now? An eight, eight and a half?"

"Eight and a half," I said. Same as the last time he'd asked.

"Bingo! I haven't lost the touch. I ran Nathan's Shoes for forty-three years," he told Maple, who nodded as if this were news. "And how tall?"

"Five seven," Mom said.

He tsked and shook his head. "Fifty-plus years ago, when they measured me for my army uniform, I was five four and a half. I shudder to think what I am now. But then, good things come in small packages, right, Nathan? I think Nathan got my shortness gene. Short but tough. The doctor says that if I watch my blood pressure and take the medication, I'll stay fine, God willing. Though not as fine as Joy." He touched my hair, which had poufed out even more as the day went on. "She's a real beauty, isn't she, Sarge?" I could see Maple trying not to smile. Sarge stood up and put his paws on Uncle Max's knees. "Ilene, not to criticize, but what have you been feeding Sarge? Sarge, you're a tub of lard." Sarge wagged his tail.

"Just what you said," Mom answered. "One cup a day of chow."

"That's the right amount," he said. "Maybe it was Mrs. Nussbaum. Did you ever meet Jack Nussbaum?

Another tub of lard, rest in peace. And Rose Nussbaum's not so slim herself. Am I right, Sarge?" Sarge's tail was wagging so hard by now, I thought it might break off. "Good thing I'm back, isn't it, boy? We're going to put you on a diet before you need a triple bypass." He gave him a scratch where the lampshade met his neck. "Run over there and show Ilene how we roll socks. It's a little trick I learned when I was in the Army. It makes a much neater ball."

I threw Maple another look. Uncle Max had a little trick for doing everything. It drove Dad up the wall. "Where's Dad?" I asked.

"Picking up a few things for dinner," Mom said.

"What for?" said Uncle Max. "I just called in an order to Broadway Gourmet. Some vegetables, some good bread, some rolls, some bagels, a nice piece of halibut."

Nathan, who even while Uncle Max talked about him had seemed totally oblivious, suddenly stopped bleeping. "I love halibut!" he said. "We never get it," he told Maple. "It's way too expensive. So's Broadway Gourmet."

"That's why there are uncles," said Uncle Max.

"When did you do that?" Mom was frowning.

"Right after lunch," he said.

"I thought you were taking a nap," she said.

"I told you I didn't need a nap. I haven't taken a nap since I was four years old."

"You could have said something before you ordered," she said. "Dinner's practically all made. We're having pasta."

"Why should you have to fuss?" he said.

"I made the sauce last night."

"It's bad enough I'm imposing on you like this. I don't want to put you out with extra cooking. Besides, I'm sure you make your sauce with salt. I'm on salt-free now. Doctor's orders. And your family likes things so salty."

I could see Mom struggling to look pleasant. "I made it without salt," she said. "Plus, if I'd known, I wouldn't have sent Marty out for the vegetables and bread."

As if on cue, the lock turned. Sarge went into his pit bull imitation. "Shut up, Sarge," Uncle Max yelled as Dad came in, lugging three bulging grocery bags. His shirt was soaking wet. "It's raining out?" said Uncle Max. Sarge continued to bark his brains out. "Sarge! At ease! He thinks he's protecting me," he explained as Sarge trotted over and lay down. "It's not supposed to rain. They didn't say anything about rain."

"Well, it's raining," Dad said. He put the bags down and wiped his face. "It started to pour just as I left the store. I picked up some ice cream for dessert."

"You shouldn't have bothered," Uncle Max said. "I got a cheesecake. Not for me. Rich foods don't agree with me anymore. But Nathan loves it. Am I right, Nathan?"

"Max just ordered a ton of groceries from Broadway Gourmet," Mom informed Dad. "I told him that was totally unnecessary."

"He got halibut, too," Nathan said. "He said that's what uncles are for."

Mom glared at him and Uncle Max. Dad rolled his eyes. I nudged Maple.

Uncle Max looked from one to the other of us. "Did I do something wrong?" he asked. "Did I commit a faux pas? If everybody's mad, I'll just call back and cancel."

"I'm not mad," Nathan said.

"I just wanted to treat everybody to a few nice things," Uncle Max said. "Now everyone's angry with me."

"We're not angry." Mom tried mightily to smile. "Don't get excited. It's not good for your blood pressure."

Uncle Max moved the walker closer and pulled himself to his feet. "Sarge, I knew we should have stayed in our own apartment," he said. His face was very red, but I couldn't tell whether it was from the effort of getting up, or because he was upset. "We were fine living on our own. We're used to each other's ways. We don't get on each other's nerves."

"You're not getting on our nerves, Max," Dad said. "It's just—"

"Good." He cut Dad off. "Because I have no intention of staying until I do. As soon as I'm back on my feet . . ."

"You just got here," Mom said. "It's a little soon to be talking about leaving."

"Could we be excused?" I said. "I have to show Maple Nathan's room. Oy, oy, oy!" I said as soon as we were in the hall. "What would you say the tension level out there is, on a scale from one to a hundred?"

"I think he's cute, in an annoying kind of way," she said.

"At least Sarge is happy," I said. "He's like a new dog, having Uncle Max back."

"So maybe it'll all be fine," she said. I made a face. "And if not, maybe they'll all kill one another and leave you in peace."

"No chance," I said. "They're far too polite and civilized."

She looked into my room. "Uh-oh!"

"What?"

She blocked my path. "You're not going to want to see this."

"Why? What'd they do?"

I looked in. You couldn't even tell it was my room. It was like I'd never lived there. They'd obliterated all traces of me. My bed was covered with Uncle Max's nubbly white bedspread, which, by itself, was not that bad, but there was a big brown corduroy bolster on it, and an incredibly hideous brown-and-orange afghan, and flannel slippers neatly lined up alongside. On the nightstand were two pairs of glasses, one of those blood pressure gizmos, a whole row of prescription bottles, and a box of tissues with a green crocheted cover. His TV was where my desk had been. There were also two big suitcases, a whole bookcase full of books, and a red plaid doggie bed. Sarge, who had followed us, stepped into it, turned around a few times, and lay down.

I was still standing there, shaking my head, listening to Sarge snuffle as he bit the fur behind his lampshade, when Mom came in. "How's it going?" I said. You could always tell how much Dad was suffering by how much he slumped. Mom just got stiffer and straighter. Right now she was looking as if she might crack in half.

"He looks okay, Uncle Max," offered Maple.

"Yeah, he does," I said. There was no way I dared even mention my room.

"Yeah, he's doing fine," Mom said. "Mr. Macho Man. He's just not in as good shape as he thinks. Which is okay, but I'm afraid I'm going to have to ask a really big favor of you, Joy. That's why I came in, so I could catch you in private."

Alarming things popped into my head. I looked at Maple.

"Joy, don't get upset," Mom said. "I can't handle another upset person around here. I'm not asking you to take care of him. I just don't feel that great about leaving him alone here all day. Not while he's still shaky. So what I'm going to need is for you to come straight home after school and stick around until Dad or I get home."

"Baby-sit Uncle Max?" I said. We were getting the match lists back next Monday. Not that I'd changed my mind about how absurd it was, but I'd had another thought after we'd come out of the girls' room that morning, which was why I'd left my hair down and spent the day pondering my image. Even if the Match Quiz was unlikely to produce Mr. Ideal Date, Mr. Male Me, Mr. Right, it could introduce me to twenty boys. Which, if you left out Justin and William and a few boring miscellaneous types in my classes, was twenty more than I knew now. All it would take was one nice one. . . . "Every day?" I asked.

"For the time being," she said. Maple shot me a look. I knew she was thinking about the match lists, too.

"Can Maple come over?"

"Of course," Mom said. "I'm not asking you to entertain him, and I don't think he'll need very much taking care of. He'll probably spend most of his time in his room. All I ask is that you don't make it seem as if you're coming home because of him. You saw how touchy he is. He'll raise holy hell if he thinks we're cramping our style because of him."

Chapter 5

Mom was right that Uncle Max didn't need much taking care of. Even with the walker, he got around pretty well. But she was dead wrong about him not wanting to be entertained. And the last thing he wanted was to stay in his room. He was right out there in the living room all the time. "It's for you, Joy," he'd say whenever the phone rang. He liked the cordless phone right by his chair so he could call Lou, his broker ("A year older than me, but still sharp as a tack"). And he always answered it before anyone could get there: "Mabel for a change."

"Mabel" called a lot because Mabel was grounded. The day Uncle Max arrived, she had another huge fight with her mom about her outfit. Mrs. Daley had two modes: pay no attention to anything Maple did, or total crackdown. This time she grounded Maple for a month, which usually meant she'd have forgotten it in a week, but until she did, Maple wasn't even allowed to come to my house. So, since Nathan had after-school clubs, afternoons were just me and Uncle Max.

The first few times Uncle Max called her Mabel, I corrected him. "Ma-*pul*," I said. "Not Ma-*bul*."

"What kind of name is Maple?" he said. "Maple's a tree's name. A person is named Mabel."

At first I thought he said things like that to be annoying. But after a few days I figured out he just had certain set things he said for every occasion. "Coffee's not too bad, if I do say so myself," he said every morning. That was after the first morning, when, after tasting Mom's coffee, he'd called Broadway Gourmet and had two pounds delivered. He was always up and dressed and at the table with his mug of coffee and the newspaper when we came in. He'd read us the weather report. Then, while we ate our Cheerios, which we were having with skim milk because that's what Mom bought for him, he'd summarize the obituaries. "Better them than me," he said. Then on to the TV schedule: "Garbage!" he'd say as he read off the listings. "Nothing but garbage." Then he and Mom would discuss his lunch choices (cottage cheese, a turkey sandwich, salt-free sardines—"I do like a good sardine"). Then he'd tuck the newspaper under his arm and push his walker to the bathroom.

He quickly developed an after-school routine, too. "Anything in the mail?" he'd ask as soon as I came in the door. He was always in his chair (formerly Dad's chair) doing the crossword puzzle. Then, after I'd taken Sarge out for his walk, he'd say, "Anything new and exciting in the outside world? You have a lot of home-work?"

I had homework every day in every subject. I'd have liked to do it in privacy, which meant the closet, since Nathan's room did not feel private, even without Nathan in it. But he invariably said, "Joy, what do you need to close yourself in there for, with no cross-ventilation? Just work here at the table. Shove the cards over. No one will bother you."

After the first few days I came straight to the table. "So," he said as soon as I'd moved his solitaire lineup and opened my binder. "What's that you're working on?"

"Math."

"I used to be good at math. I was always a straight-A student." He pulled himself up and came over with his puzzle. I pushed the stop button on the Walkman as he sat down next to me. "You do your math in pen?" I nodded. "Is that wise?"

"I don't know. A pen's what was handy." Dad would have pointed out that he was doing his puzzle in pen, but I knew that wasn't wise.

"Go over and get yourself a pencil." I did, and wrote out the first equation. "You don't happen to know a

Biblical gemstone?" he asked before I could start solving it. "Six letters?" I shook my head. "Never mind. I got it."

The problems were hard. All my homework looked hard, so I began drawing a lumpy, Sarge-like dog on the inside of my binder. "I thought you were supposed to be working," he said.

"I'm easing into it," I said.

He peered over his glasses at the drawing. "What's that supposed to be?"

I quickly gave it pointy ears and whiskers. "A cat."

"I hate to tell you, it looks more like a dog. It's very cute, though. I never knew you were such an artist."

"Yeah, well . . ." I was always pleased when people liked my silly drawings. It was only Kestrel I kept private.

"If you're really still easing in," he asked, "could I interest you maybe in a quick game of gin rummy?" He won, as always, and one game turned into best of five, and then he had a card trick to show me, and then there was the story that went with the card trick, and then, when Nathan came home, he wanted us to show the card trick to Nathan. And that's how my afternoons went.

On the days Mom had class, I got dinner started. "So, anything new and exciting in the outside world?"

he asked as soon as we'd all sat down at the table. "How was work?"

"The usual," Dad said.

"Tiring," said Mom.

"Anything I can do to help out?" he asked.

"It's not necessary," Mom said. "But thanks anyway."

Except when Nathan and I got into something, that tended to be the level of our dinner conversations. One night, during a lull, I told them about the Match Quiz. "Match Quiz?" he said. "That's like in my parents' day. Years back, that was a common thing, you know, matchmaking. Arranged marriages. There was a whole musical about it. *Hello, Dolly!* Ilene, remember when we went to see that on Broadway?"

"This is nothing like that, Max," Dad said. "Joy's just starting high school." Mom stopped cutting the skin off her chicken long enough to give him a look. She and Dad had been giving each other a lot of looks this week.

"My mother was barely fifteen when she got married," said Uncle Max. "That was for all intents and purposes an arranged marriage."

"I'm not trying to get married," I said, sorry I'd brought it up. "I probably won't even meet anybody."

"Sure you will." He glanced over at Mom's plate.

"You're not going to throw that skin away, are you? It's the best part. Pass it over here."

"It's not good for you," Mom said.

"Just give it to him, Ilene," Dad said.

It never got as tense as that first halibut night, but I sometimes thought Nathan and I were having an easier time adjusting to him than they were.

Adjusting to Nathan's room, though, was not easy. He was pretty good about not talking to me, and he never practiced the drums when I was there. But he insisted on falling asleep with his Top 40 music going, his mice scratched and scrabbled all night long, he pissed and moaned about getting up so he could take Sarge for his morning walk, and within two days, his junk— Magic Cards, marbles, stray puzzle pieces, old homework—was migrating over to my side.

I tried to deal with it by spending no waking time in there. As soon as we'd cleaned up from dinner each night, I headed for the closet. Dad had put a little fan in for me, so I could close the door almost all the way without sweltering. I stayed in there—doing homework, drawing, talking to Maple—till they'd all gone to bed. Mornings, I tried to be out of Nathan's room before he woke up, which wasn't hard, since the mice always got me up way before the alarm. Saturday, Maple's mom let me come over, and I stayed through dinner. And Nathan had made a new friend at school, so he spent all of Sunday over there. So the weekend didn't go too badly, though Mom and Dad continued to flip-flop between borderline testy, being overly careful of Uncle Max's feelings, and acting as if he weren't there.

Monday morning, Uncle Max was smiling when I came in to breakfast. "Look at this, Joy," he said, pointing to the cane hooked on the edge of the table. "Things are looking up! I made it in here without the walker!"

"That's great," I said. Maybe that meant pretty soon he wouldn't need me around all the time. Maybe he'd even be able to go out and do things on his own.

"Enough with the walker, right, Sarge?" he said. Sarge was in his usual spot under the table, hoping a few stray Cheerios would fall his way. "It doesn't suit our image."

"I didn't know Sarge had an image," Dad said.

Uncle Max spooned up a prune. "What are you, kidding? Sarge is a mighty hunter, right, boy?" Dad raised his eyebrows. "You laugh. Terriers are world-class ratters. You didn't know that? That's what they were bred for. You think cats are good mousers? Sarge sees a rat ..." He bared his teeth and growled, then opened his jaws wide and snapped them on the prune.

"He better not touch Kurt and Ludwig!" Nathan said.

"Don't worry," Dad said. "Sarge wouldn't notice Kurt and Ludwig if they were sitting in his bowl."

"Don't be so sure," Uncle Max said. "There's plenty of life in the old boy." He looked over at Mom. "I thought a little later I might try to walk down and get the mail. If it goes well, tomorrow I'll take Sarge out for his walk."

"Don't push it, Max, please," she said. "You haven't been out at all yet, never mind alone."

He made a face. "I'm not used to being cooped up like this all day. It's pretty sad when you can't even take your dog out to do its business."

"If you wait till after school, I can go down with you," I said.

"Anyway," Mom said, "we're going somewhere this afternoon, remember? I'm taking you to the doctor."

"Whoopdedoo," he said.

For me, though, this was great news. I couldn't wait to get to the bus stop to tell Maple. We'd spent much of Saturday trying to work out a plan for Match Day, but since we'd figured we were basically both grounded, we hadn't gotten very far. Now I was free!

I was just getting up to leave when Nathan said, "Hey, Joy, I forgot to tell you. Ben's brother says he knows you from school."

"Who's Ben?" I got an apple from the fridge and put it in my backpack.

"My friend. The one whose house I went to. I think

he likes you. He kept asking me all these, like, personal questions."

My heart fluttered. I ran down the list of every boy in any of my classes who'd paid the slightest attention to me. There were several who weren't terrible. "Who is he? What's his name?"

"Justin," he said.

"I've always liked the name Justin," said Mom.

But I had a bad feeling. "Justin *what*?"

"Zuwadski," said Nathan. "Ben's name is Zuwadski. I'm pretty sure he's going to call and ask you out. I told him our phone number. I said you're always here. What, bad move?" he asked, as I grabbed my throat and began making gagging noises.

"Maybe it's a sign from God," I told Maple at the bus stop. I'd given her the old good news/bad news routine. "I mean, out of hundreds of thousands of sixth-grade boys in the city of New York, Nathan picks Justin Zuwadski's brother as his friend? What is this telling me? That I should just bow to the inevitable? I shouldn't even bother with the Match Quiz?"

"Or that you should say no if he asks you out?" she said, looking at me the way Mom did when I got what she called "excited."

"It's not even Justin," I said, realizing now why this was getting to me. "Justin may be a wonderful human being." She wrinkled her nose. "You're right," I said, "but that's not even the point. It's that he's everything we're trying to get away from. He's junior high school personified—goofy, geeky, gawky, obnoxious, nerdy, uncool . . ." She gave me her okay-I-get-it look. "I don't care, Maple, I didn't make it all the way up here to have my first date in life be with a bigger version of my brother."

Chapter 6

All anybody talked about all day was the Match Quiz. And all day I seesawed between dread and excitement. But Justin didn't say a word to me at school, and my list, which I got at the end of eighth period, was Justin-free. In fact, I knew no one on it.

"Now what?" Maple said. A lot of kids were going around to different homerooms to hunt down list people, but luckily even she agreed that walking up to some unknown person and saying, "Hi there, are you my match?" was too scary. There was also the small matter of her being grounded. So we headed to her apartment, to see if we could get up the nerve to make some calls.

I don't know if it was having the lists, or not having to go home, or the box of Dunkin' Donuts we bought to give us courage, but walking down Broadway, wiping cinnamon sugar and jelly off our faces, everything suddenly felt fun, or funny or both. I kept seeing guys looking at us: the Dunkin' Donuts man, boys on the street, the men digging up a sidewalk. As we crossed the street, a man in a beer truck called out something that sounded like "Shake that thing!"

"Tell me he's not talking about me!" I said. I began slowing down each time we passed one of those big mirrors outside Love Cosmetics to see if my pants were too tight or if I was walking strangely.

"Just look straight ahead and frown," said Maple. "Don't make eye contact. Act normal."

"If I knew how to do that . . ." I said.

"Come on, Joy," she said. "You're acting like you just landed on the planet."

"So, are we really going to do this?" I asked, once we'd made it to her house and were settled on her bed. Of the twelve donuts, five were left. We were both slightly ill but definitely still giddy.

"Yeah." She reached into her backpack. "Here's our script."

"You wrote out a script?" I kicked off my sneakers.

"Last night. So we wouldn't be nervous." She handed it to me.

" 'Hello, blank, my name is blank,' " I read in a Wilma Flintstone voice, " 'and I got your name—' We're not really going to say this?"

"Why not? What would *you* say?"

"I don't know. Something less boring."

"Like what?"

" 'Hi, this is Maple from Victoria's Secret, calling to confirm your lingerie order?' "

"Tacky," she said.

"There's always the old 'Hello, is your refrigerator running?' "

"Joy. We're not in the fifth grade. This is serious. What's wrong with my script?"

But I couldn't give it up. "How about 'Hello, this is the front desk. Your iguanas have arrived?' "

"Okay, smartass. Go for it." She handed me the phone.

"Me?" It came out a squeak. Where was the smartass when I needed her?

"Uh-huh."

I sat there staring at the list, waiting for an inspiration.

"What are you doing?" she asked after a while.

"Trying to figure this out." Kami was a cool name. Max definitely was not. But did I start out with someone promising or practice on the uncool ones? "I mean, how do you tell anything from a list of names, numbers, and homerooms?"

"Here, give me your list," she said. I handed it to her. "Adam Urbach," she said.

"He sounds good to you?"

"I don't know. He's a ninth grader and A's at the top of the alphabet. You can practice on him."

"What will I say?" I was still squeaking. This was

ridiculous. Why was my heart pounding like this over calling someone I didn't even know just because he happened to have filled out the same twenty inane questions?

"Say anything," she said. "Just do it. Now."

I dialed, but hung up before anyone could answer. "Would you go first?" I said.

"Okay," she said. "Give me the phone. I'm starting right at the top." She patted her hair, arranged her face, and dialed. "Good afternoon." She cleared her throat. "Wade Allen, please. Oh, hi." Her voice brightened. She was smiling. "This is Maple Daley. Yeah! From school. Uh-huh, from the list!"

Why was I such a jellyfish? I reached over and pushed speaker phone. "I never thought someone would really call," I heard Wade say. He had a nice, deep voice.

"Yeah, but now what happens?" she asked.

"I dunno," he said. "That's why I didn't call anybody." Then the conversation died until he said, "So, should we, like, meet?"

She made a mock-panicked face. Even I felt a little flash of panic. "Sure," she said. "When?"

"Well, I work most afternoons," he said. "I, like, pick up this little kid at school. But tomorrow I don't have to stay with him, just drop him off at home. Is tomorrow good? He lives right near the West Side

Barnes and Noble. I could meet you there, like, three thirty."

"But you're grounded," I mouthed.

She waved that away. "How will I know who you are?"

"I'll be the person in the long raincoat," he said. "How will I know you?"

"I'll be the person with the blue hair on top."

"Cool!" he said. I couldn't believe how easily this was going. "I tried mine blue once, but it came out a sickly color."

"Yeah, if you don't bleach it enough first, it doesn't work. What color is it?"

"It *was* brown," he said. "Before I took the razor to it."

"I can't believe you got a date on your first try," I said when she hung up the phone. "How'd you do that?"

"It's a gift," she said. Her face darkened. "You're coming with me when I meet him, right? I'm not doing this alone."

"I'll be there," I said. "But what are you going to do about your mom?"

"I'll tell her something. Here." She handed me my list. "Start calling. We've gotta find somebody for you."

"Okay," I said. "I'll try Urbach, then Morales." But

the instant she handed me the phone, my hands went clammy again and my voice stuck in my throat. "I don't know what to say," I said.

"What about all your good ideas?"

"I can only think of them when it doesn't count," I said.

"Then just say 'Hi, this is Joy,' " she said. "Wade knew who I was. Come on, it's really easy. Don't wimp out on me now." I sat there wimpishly. "Want me to call and say I'm you?"

"No," I said.

"So then what are you going to do, wait for someone to call you? I thought we decided that was passive and cowardly."

I'd never known if I was a brave person or a coward, but I'd always assumed that when put to the test, I'd measure up. It's just that this was the wrong sort of test. "I'll call tomorrow," I said. "Or look for people after school. I may be free, if Uncle Max's doctor visit went well. Plus, by tomorrow, I might be braver."

"Tomorrow we're meeting Wade," she said.

Mom was in the living room going through the mail when I got home. Dad called out hello, but Uncle Max barely looked up from his paper, though Sarge had rushed over as soon as I came in the door. "So how'd it go?" Mom asked as I dropped my backpack on the chair. "Did you find a match?"

"Not unless somebody called," I said. "But Maple has a date." I'd spent the whole walk home bouncing back and forth between being furious at myself, telling myself I didn't need a match, and wishing I'd meet somebody like Wade. I followed Mom into the kitchen to see what I could work out for tomorrow afternoon. She seemed really tight and tired. "Is everything okay?" I asked.

"Everything's fine," she said, pouring herself a glass of wine.

She didn't usually drink on weekdays. "Is Uncle Max okay?" I asked. "He seemed kind of weird just now. He hardly even said hello."

She took a big swallow. "I think he's a little upset."

"Why? What'd the doctor say?"

"He said he was coming along. But I guess Max thought he was going to tell him he could go back to his apartment, and of course he didn't."

I didn't like how her voice sounded. I sat down at the counter. "What'd he say about it, the doctor?"

She took another sip, then opened the drawer and began looking through a pile of takeout menus. "Well, he said what we're doing is just great, that basically, this is the best place for him, here, with his family."

"So then he has to stay here," I said.

"Joy"—she didn't look at me—"you know he has to stay here."

"But did he say he couldn't be alone?" My timing was terrible, but it was a fair question. I needed to know. "Did he say we had to stay with him all the time?"

She turned to face me. "It's only been a week, Joy," she said. "I really think you can hang in there a little longer without it killing you." She handed me the take-out menu. "Here. Decide what you want. I figured if we get Chinese it might cheer us up."

It didn't. The good part was that no one asked anything about my afternoon, and that Nathan wasn't there to bring up Justin, but what happened was just as uncomfortable.

"Ilene," Dad said, almost as soon as our food had arrived, "have you seen my mug?"

"Your beer mug?" she asked.

"The one I use every night," he said.

"Did you look in the cabinet?" she asked.

"It's not there," he said. "And it's not in the dishwasher."

Uncle Max put down his spare rib. "The one with the big chip in it?" he said. "I threw it out."

"You threw it out? Without asking?" Dad's voice rose.

"You have another one exactly like it," said Uncle Max. "I didn't want you to hurt yourself."

"It's not exactly like it," Dad said. "And I've been using it that way for the last ten years."

"Max," Mom looked hard at Dad. "Marty doesn't

mean to snap at you. He knows you were just trying to help—"

"I didn't snap," Dad snapped. "I very carefully and deliberately didn't snap. But he has to—"

"The reason it got chipped," said Uncle Max, "is that you put it in the dishwasher."

"Why does that matter, now that you've thrown it out?" said Dad.

"I'm just telling you so that you don't chip the other one."

"I don't like the other one," said Dad. "That's why I don't use it. I liked that one." He sounded just like Nathan.

"Well, maybe it's still in the garbage," said Mom. "I can look."

"If I knew what a hubbub I'd be causing . . ." said Uncle Max. I saw Dad flinch. "I'm sorry, but I put the garbage out already. It had all those shrimp shells in it."

"So there were no calls at all for me this afternoon?" I said. "No hang-ups or wrong numbers, no strange messages?"

"No one but Lou," Uncle Max said. "The market was off another eighty points today, but he keeps telling me I shouldn't get excited. I'm not excited. Everything else seems to be going downhill, why shouldn't the market?"

"Max, don't feel that way," said Mom.

My calls were clearly not uppermost in their minds. "If anyone does happen to call," I said, "make sure you write it down, okay? And get their names. In fact, maybe we should just keep the machine on all the time. Lots of people do that so they don't have to be bothered."

I saw Mom look at Uncle Max to make sure now I hadn't hurt his feelings, too. "That's hardly necessary," she said. "Max will be happy to take your calls."

Chapter 7

What I ended up doing the next day, since there was no way I could have brought it up the night before, was calling from the street and telling Uncle Max I'd be about an hour late. With no Mom around to veto it, he said it was fine.

"Are you as tense as I am?" Maple asked now as we walked to Barnes and Noble. "I'm sweating, I'm so nervous."

I was fine at the moment, having narrowly escaped Justin on the way out. "You're sweating 'cause it's eighty degrees out," I said. She was wearing a neon green hairy sweater, a short denim skirt, thick red tights with white fishnet stockings over them, and heavy boots. "Take off your sweater."

"I'll feel too naked. Plus it'll mess up my hair." She patted her barrette arrangement. "He probably won't even show up." She stopped walking. "Why am I making this into a big thing? Worst case, we do the Match

Mixer next week, right? It's our fallback. If I hate Wade, and all else fails, we'll just go to the mixer."

That got me nervous. I'd been so busy thinking about my list yesterday and walking around today hoping to spot people, and wondering where I was going to get the nerve to start calling, it hadn't really sunk in that there was a mixer. That was a whole other thing to start thinking about. "You'll like Wade," I said.

"What if he doesn't like me?" she said.

"Then he's too dumb to live."

Wade was already standing outside Barnes and Noble when we got there. There was no missing him: a skinny, six-foot-three person with a shaved head and a long raincoat. He bounded over to Maple and shook her hand, then mine.

"I wasn't sure you'd come," said Maple.

"I didn't think you would either," he said. Wade wasn't handsome. A lot of people would have called him funny looking. His nose was too big and his neck too long. But I liked him instantly.

I could see she did, too. "What do you want to do?" she said, looking up at him.

"Get ice cream?" he said. "When in doubt, get ice cream."

"I like ice cream," Maple said. "Want some ice cream, Joy?"

There was an ice-cream store right up the street. I got what I always get: a root-beer float with mint chocolate chip. Wade and Maple, it turned out, both loved Heath Bar crunch. Over the next half hour, as we walked on Broadway, they discovered they both also loved strawberries, hated MTV, and had obnoxious mothers. Maple looked really short walking next to him. A short multicolored person next to a tall, no-color person. But there it was. There was no mistaking it: a Match.

"What do you think?" she whispered when Wade went over to a trash can to dump his cup.

"I like him," I whispered back. "He's great."

"This match thing is incredible," she said. "It really works! Do you believe it? It's amazing! He's so nice! I can't stop smiling."

Her face did look a bit out of control. But then so did his. I almost felt like I was eavesdropping, watching them. "I better go," I said.

All I could think about the whole way home was meeting someone like that. But there was no way I was going to call anyone all by myself. And no one called me that night except Maple. "Guess what!" she said. "I'm ungrounded! I, like, totally groveled, and Mom ungrounded me, so we're going out Friday night, me and Wade. Do you believe this? He already asked me. I am so happy. We're probably going to a movie. You can come, you know, he won't mind, he said he liked you. Joy, wouldn't it be great if you met someone, and we could double?"

I did meet someone the next morning. It happened during Spanish. Señor Rosen had just called on me to conjugate the preterit of *hacer.* I was sitting there reveling in not having screwed it up when the girl behind me handed me a note. "Dear Señorita Cooper," it read. "I think you are on my match list. Richard Quinn." My heart knocked. I turned around. A very good-looking person with glasses nodded and sort of half smiled/half frowned at me. I smiled back. I hadn't realized this guy was on my list because Señor Rosen always gave his name the Spanish pronunciation: Señor Keen. He caught up with me as I headed for the door. "So what do you think about this match thing?" he asked. He was taller than I'd thought, and even better looking.

"You're taller than you look sitting down," I said. Oy! Get this girl some social skills!

But it didn't seem to turn him off. "Are you going to the cafeteria?" he asked.

"Sure," I said. "If you can wait a minute."

"Listen, will you feel abandoned if I have a lunch date?" I asked Maple, who was waiting for me on the first floor. "I can't tell yet, but he looks promising."

"Go for it!" she said. "I'll make sure I sit close enough so I can keep tabs."

Señor Keen ate a peanut-butter sandwich he'd brought from home. He said he always brought his lunch because the cafeteria didn't always have peanut butter. And for the next half hour, we discussed peanut butter—the A to Z of peanut butter: crunchy compared to superchunk, store brand versus Skippy, health food peanut butter with a pool of grease on top, grind-it-yourself peanut butter.

"Well, if there's anything you ever want to know about peanut butter, Señor Keen's your man," I told Maple afterward, trying not to sound too disappointed.

"You can't give up on him," she said. "He's too cute. He must have other interests."

"Yeah, jelly," I said.

"Come on, Joy, did you even try to draw him out?"

"Oh, yes! I asked if he knew the Spanish word for peanut. He said it was *cacahuete.*"

"*Caca-whooey?*"

"He asked if I'd eat with him tomorrow."

Her face brightened. "He likes you! That's so cool. What'd you tell him?"

"I told him I had to eat with you."

"You didn't have to do that," she said.

"Don't look at me like that," I said. "This was not a match."

We met someone else that afternoon: the famous Adam Urbach, the person I didn't have the nerve to call. He was a tall, thin kid with headphones and big pants. "Hey, Joy, man!" He sort of bumbled over to me in the hall. "You're Joy, right?" I nodded. He turned to the kid behind him. "See, told you so! I told you that was her." He laughed goofily. "What's up, Joyful? You don't care if I call you that?"

What was up was he was stoned. "Yeah, I do," I said.

"You could have given him a chance," Maple said, when he'd stumbled off again, still giggling. "He's not that bad. I'm sure he's not smoked all the time."

"Hey, if that's my match . . ." I said.

The next day, I met a junior, Chris. He was so suave I was really psyched when he asked me to meet him in the park. When I got there, though, I found out he had assembled twelve of the twenty girls from his match list, not to mention four of his friends. "We're just, like, trying to get an overview of this whole match thing," he said. Chris was a jerk, but a couple of the girls seemed really nice.

That night, though, someone called just as we were finishing dinner. Dad got it.

"Boy for you."

"Bet it's Justin!" said Nathan, who'd been at the Zuwadskis' again.

But it turned out to be somebody named Dave, and he had a nice voice. Heart racing in spite of myself, I took the phone into the closet. He said he was a sophomore. He worked on the school paper. He offered to meet me the next day, after he got done. "Hold on a minute," I told him. I ran into the living room, where Dad was taking the last of the dishes to the kitchen while Mom wiped the table. "Listen," I said, "is it all right if I don't come straight home tomorrow afternoon?" I told them about Dave. "Nathan doesn't have after-school, so he can watch Uncle Max for me."

At that instant, Uncle Max came through the kitchen door. "What are you talking about, 'watch Uncle Max'?" he said, scowling.

I looked at Mom for help.

"Nothing," she said. Mom's a pathetic liar.

"Since when does Uncle Max need watching?" he demanded. "Ilene, have you been making Joy come home from school to take care of me? Is that the deal?"

Mom looked at Dad. I could see he'd decided to stay out of it. "It's just for the time being," she said. "I mean, doesn't it seem like a good idea, just till you're—"

Uncle Max cut her off. "You think I need a baby-sitter?"

"No, of course not. That's not what anybody means—"

"Because if I'm so doddering I need your children to baby-sit me, you should put me in a home."

"You're not doddering." Mom was looking more and more flustered. "That's not it at all."

"In that case, Joy," he looked at me, "you go right back and tell this young man you can go."

I didn't know what to do. This was not fair, putting me in the middle. On the other hand, I knew exactly what he felt like, trying to stand up to her. Meanwhile, poor Dave was still on hold.

"Listen, Dave," I said when I got back to the closet. "Could we, like, maybe do this another time? I've got some things to work out first."

"That's cool," he said, but he said it so quickly I knew that as soon as he hung up he was going to call the next girl on his list.

"So are you going?" Uncle Max asked when I came out. Mom was at her desk, pretending to grade papers. I saw her back stiffen.

"Nah," I said. "He didn't sound that great."

"You didn't turn him down because of me?"

I shook my head. "It wasn't 'cause of you." I was no better at lying than Mom.

"I hate to tell you guys," he said to Mom's back. "The one around here who needs the matchmaker isn't Joy. It's me."

Chapter 8

I was by myself the next day after school when Justin Zuwadski appeared at my locker. "I see you're still into crustacean jewelry," he said, touching my ear. "Are you gonna go to that Match Mixer next Friday?"

Here it was. The moment I'd been dreading. And Maple was with Wade. "I don't know," I said. I noticed he'd started gelling up his hair. He was wearing a pale green, sort of shrunken nylon shirt. The way it stretched tightly across his stomach made me think of a melon ball.

"We could, like, maybe go together, if you want," he said.

"Doesn't that sort of, like, defeat the purpose?" I asked.

"What purpose?"

"The purpose of mixing. Of getting to meet your matches. Of meeting people you don't already know." I didn't want to come right out and hurt his feelings.

Not that Justin seemed overly sensitive, but he *was* attempting this image change. Then I had the horrible thought that he might say something like "I'd like to know *you* better," so I quickly added, "Anyway, I don't dance," which I thought sounded more dignified than "I can't dance." Then, to put one last nail in the coffin, I said, "Besides, I have to be at home almost all the time to take care of my uncle."

There was a colossal racket coming from Nathan's room when I got home. "Ben's over," Uncle Max said. "He brought his guitar and amplifier. Between that and the drums, I'm surprised the neighbors haven't called."

"The Curse of the Zuwadskis," I said, heading to the kitchen.

"It was worse before," he said, following me. "I made them turn it down. Poor Sarge has gone into hiding. He thinks it's an enemy attack. So anything new and exciting today?" he asked. I'd wondered if he'd still be upset from last night, but he seemed back to normal. "How's the match business?"

"Bad," I said. But not nearly as bad as the thought of going to the mixer with Justin. I was right about him not being thin skinned. It had taken at least ten minutes for him to notice he was being rejected.

"So you didn't hear anything more from that Dave fellow?"

"No." I took out the juice. "I'm considering becoming a hermit."

"No, you're not," he said. "You're just discouraged. It's his loss, you know. I'll take some of that juice, too." He opened the dishwasher and took out two glasses. "Shake it up first. You meet any of the others?"

"Well"—I shook it up—"there was Señor *Cacahuete,* Herb Man, and Dr. Bunsen Honeydew."

He chuckled. "A doctor, eh? This match business can't be that terrible, if you've landed a doctor."

"Not a doctor. A Muppet," I said. "Who wasn't even on my list. And he landed on me!"

"Well, maybe I can cheer you up," he said. "You got a couple nibbles just now."

My heart raced. "Someone called? Why didn't you tell me?"

"What do you think I'm doing? Actually," his eyes shone. "It was three someones. Just a minute. Let me go get the pad." He picked up his cane. I followed him back to the living room. Excruciating bangs and bleats and blats were still coming from Nathan's room. "So the first young man's name is Kevin Rossi," he said.

"And is he calling back?" I asked.

"Nah," he shook his head, "I had to rule him out."

"What?"

"I told him you were fourteen years old and he should find someone more his age."

I couldn't believe this. "You asked how old he was?"

"You bet I did. He said he was almost seventeen. For all I know, he's been left back."

Why did nothing around here ever go easily? "Listen," I said. "Uncle Max. All you have to do is take the messages, write down their names. You don't even have to get their numbers. I have them on my list. You don't have to interview them or screen them for me. Okay?" He nodded, but it was a lost cause. I knew it. "So who else called?"

"He had sort of a thick accent."

"Was it Kami, or maybe Rajiv?"

"Could have been Kami, but I wrote down the number, so you can find him on your list. However, you might not need to call him back. I haven't told you about the third boy yet." By now he had a positively impish gleam in his eye. "You know the story of Goldilocks and the three bears? Remember how she tried the porridge? The first one was too hot, the second one was too cold, and the third one was just right?"

"The third one was Dr. Bunsen Honeydew," I reminded him.

"Then never mind. At any rate, this one's name is Max."

"Max?" That was the first name I'd eliminated.

"I said the same thing. I said, '*My* name is Max. I didn't know they named kids that anymore. I asked him if it was short for Maxwell or Maximilian. I'm Maxwell, you know. They went in for very English-sounding names in those days. Maxwell, Milton, Mortimer. He's just plain Max. It's a very in name these days, he tells me. He sounded like a serious young man. So I asked him a few questions. He's in the tenth grade, he said, which sounds fine, and he asked me a few things about you."

I groaned. Another disaster in the making. "Like what?"

"This and that. Anyway, his mother teaches science, his father's a clinical psychologist, so with any luck, he isn't crazy, and he sounded nice. They live right around the corner from the store—"

"Did you find out what size shoes he wears, too?"

"We didn't get that personal."

"That better mean you didn't say anything about me."

"Just that you're smart and witty and a pleasure to behold."

"Oy vey!" I said. "Uncle Max!"

"Don't get your shorts in a knot! I didn't put it in those exact words. I tried not to say anything that would embarrass you. I just said he'd made a brilliant choice, calling you. Listen, Joy." His face turned serious. "Getting back to this Dave fellow. We both know your mother's going overboard with the nursemaid bit, but there's no point arguing with her, right? It doesn't work."

I nodded.

"But this doesn't mean I have to crap up your life," he went on. "We just have to be a little clever about it."

"What does that mean?" I wasn't sure what I was hearing.

"It means we go along as best we can, play by the rules, and where possible, I try to help you out. You get my drift?"

A minute ago, I'd felt like shaking him. I still sort of did, but I also had the sudden urge to hug him.

"So listen." Now he was really smiling. "I told Max to come over here at six o'clock tomorrow night. This way we all get to look him over, make sure he's not a dope fiend or an ax murderer. If you don't like him, I'll just signal Ilene to call you in for dinner. And if you like him, you'll go out somewhere."

"How will you know?" I said.

"Please." He gave me a look. "Give me a little credit. Trust me, darling. A boy named Max, what could be bad? This could be a match."

Chapter 9

"So what do you think, Goldilocks?" Maple asked me the next morning as we got to school. "Think he'll show up in a brown suit, and that he's short and bald and says 'Am I right?'"

"Hey, I'm supposed to be the pessimist," I said. "You're supposed to say, 'Oh, Joy, don't be ridiculous. He'll be great. You'll love him.'"

"He'll be great," she said. "You'll love him. See?" She pointed to a tall, suave, seniory-looking person lounging by the wall. "That's Max, right over there."

"Right. Unless that's Max." I pointed to a skanky-looking boy bent under a gigantic backpack, then to a punky person with a ring in his lip, then to a Zuwadski wannabe. "Or that. Or that."

"It's so weird Wade doesn't know him," she said.

"Could be because he's a figment of Uncle Max's imagination," I said.

"We'll soon find out," she said.

We'd decided last night that Maple and Wade would come home with me. If by some miracle Max turned out to be nice, the four of us would do something together. If, as seemed more likely, he was a dud, either they or Uncle Max would ease him out the door. Having a plan definitely helped. But the day still felt endless. I couldn't stop scanning the halls, scrutinizing faces. There were so many boys here. Lots of them looked possible, but were any of them on my match list? Were any of them Max? Mom had agreed to let me go to Maple's after school, so at least I didn't have to spend the afternoon at home waiting nervously. But by the time we met Wade outside the building where he baby-sat, I was pretty antsy.

Not as antsy, it turned out, as Uncle Max. "It's five to six already," he said, when we came in the door. "Where were you? I was starting to get worried. I put out a few little snacks and tidied up. Your dad got out early, so he's taking a nap, and Nathan's in his room with Ben. I told them no drums today. Ilene's in the kitchen. They've all promised to stay out of your hair. Come," he said to Wade and Maple. "Make yourselves comfortable. Sit down." He took my arm and led me aside. "I hope this Max isn't as far out as your friends," he whispered. "Maple I'm already used to, but who's this bald scarecrow she's with?"

"His name is Wade," I said. "And don't embarrass her!"

"Don't worry," he said.

"And don't call her Mabel, either. Okay?"

"That was a joke." He gave my arm a pat. "I'll be very proper and low profile. See what I did to the living room?" He beamed. "I thought I might find the vacuuming a little strenuous, but it was fine." He'd also plumped up the sofa cushions, picked up Sarge's bones, put away all the books and magazines, made the papers on Mom's desk into a neat pile, and set out a bowl of mixed nuts, a dish of celery and olives, and a plate of cheese and crackers. "I was going to get pistachios, but they only had the red ones, and I thought you wouldn't want your fingers all red. Pardon my asking," he said to Wade, once we were all sitting. "What's with the raincoat?"

"You never know when it's going to rain," Wade said.

Uncle Max threw me a look. So it goes for proper and low profile, I thought. But before he could say anything, Mom came in. I knew I could count on Mom to be proper, even though her eyes narrowed at the long, wrinkled raincoat. But Maple had barely gotten through the introductions when Sarge jumped up and started barking.

My stomach gave a lurch.

"Aha! He hears the elevator," said Uncle Max. "Perfect. Right on time. Ilene, that's your cue to disappear." Mom obeyed. The doorbell rang. I looked at Maple.

"So you going to answer it?" said Uncle Max.

I went to the door, gave Maple one last look, and opened it.

"I'm Max," said Max.

"I'm Joy," I said. So far, so good. He was not wearing a brown suit; he was not skanky, roly-poly, or Zuwadskiesque. In fact, he looked really nice, a little taller than me, dark eyes and hair, and just on the funky side of normal—enough to be interesting but not so outthere Uncle Max would make comments. I didn't know if I was supposed to shake his hand, but he kept his in his pockets. He looked almost as nervous as I was. "I guess you should come in," I said.

"Yeah, sure," he said.

But the instant he set foot in the foyer, Sarge hurled himself at him, barking his brains out. "Down, boy!" Uncle Max shouted from the living room. "Don't be scared," he called as Sarge fastened himself to Max's leg. "He's never bitten anyone." But Sarge wasn't biting Max. He was sniffing, whuffling, circling him, smelling his feet, his legs. Then his paws were up on Max's pants, his snout between Max's legs.

"Get down, Sarge!" I shouted. Sarge did not get

down. I could have grabbed his lampshade and yanked his nose out of Max's crotch, but it was too embarrassing.

Uncle Max hurried in, followed by Wade, Maple, and Mom. "Sarge, down!" Mom cried. "Max, I'm terribly sorry! Down, you bad dog!"

"Sarge!" Uncle Max grabbed Sarge's collar. "Behave yourself. Lie down!" He shoved him down. "I apologize," he said to Max. "He never jumps on people. Sarge, what's gotten into you?"

Now Dad appeared, looking rumpled and out of sorts, as he always did after a nap. "What's all the shouting?" he said. Then, as he took it in, "Sarge, are you a horny hound?"

"Who's a horny hound? What's going on?" asked Nathan. Now everyone was here, even Ben.

"Sarge seems to be in love," said Uncle Max. "As a rule, he doesn't like strangers," he told Max. "You should be honored. He's very particular who he sniffs."

"Uh, this goes beyond sniffing," said Dad.

"Maybe he smells my cats." Max spoke slowly and distinctly, as if he'd suddenly found himself in a loony bin and didn't want to rile the inmates.

"How many cats does your family have, Max?" Mom asked in her hostess voice.

"Three." He squatted beside Sarge, no doubt so he wouldn't have to look at us, and began scratching him on the belly. Sarge's hind leg twitched. I could see Maple trying not to crack up. I didn't know whether to giggle, cry, or run.

Uncle Max gave me his hold-your-horses look. "Ilene," he said, "why don't we go into my room and watch the six o'clock news. Sarge, you're coming with us. Nathan, you and Ben can go back to your room."

So they all left, and we went to the living room. Maple and Wade sat down on the couch. I took Uncle Max's chair. Max chose the straight chair farthest from me.

"Well, that was exciting," Maple said.

Max didn't say anything, but if one was comfortable and ten was desperate to escape, I'd have put him at eight and a half.

I tried to think of conversational openers: So, Max, would you describe your ideal date as dinner and a movie, bungee jumping, or being humped by a geriatric dog? I should have gone to the bathroom as soon as I got home. Now I didn't dare leave. Wade took Maple's hand. "Would anybody like some cheese?" I said.

"No, thanks," said Max.

I sat watching Wade rub his thumb around on Maple's palm. Max was edging up toward nine. When Nathan reappeared, I was almost glad. "Does anyone here know anything about mice?" he asked. " 'Cause

Ben and I are going to use Kurt Cobain and Ludwig for our science project, and we could use some help figuring out these plans."

Max suddenly sprang to life. "What's the project?" he asked.

"We're building a hamster-powered airplane," said Nathan.

"Since when?" I said. This was news to me.

"Since Ben downloaded the plans off the Internet," he said.

"I think I read about that," Max said. "It was in *The Amateur Scientist*, right?" Nathan nodded. "I've tried a couple of their projects. They're great."

We were evidently all relieved Nathan was back.

"What I'm wondering is," Nathan said, "the plans say hamsters. Think it'll work with mice?"

"No reason why not," Max said.

"Want to see?" Nathan asked him.

"Is that cool?" Max asked me. It was pretty much the first time he'd made eye contact since the Sarge attack.

"Sure, go ahead," I said.

"We just have to close the door, in case Sarge gets loose," Nathan said. Maple snickered. "It's not just that," he said. "He's a world-class ratter, Uncle Max says."

I looked at Maple. "Why don't you go with them, Wade?" she said.

"Get me out of here!" I told her as soon as they were gone.

"Why? He's really cute," she said. "I love those classy eyebrows, and those dark, brooding eyes."

"Yeah, he's brooding about how he got himself roped into this. It's a disaster. He hasn't even looked at me."

"He's probably just shy," she said. "Or embarrassed, one. I mean, it's not every day—"

"He isn't shy with Nathan." I wondered if I had bad breath, or if I smelled. Or was it just my family?

"Stop looking like that," she said. "What do you want to do?"

"Climb down the fire escape before he gets back?"

She actually looked at the windows. "You don't have a fire escape."

"Exactly," I said.

"I'm serious," she said. "Do you want us to stick around, or should we try all going out? He might be more comfortable somewhere else."

I nodded. "Probably anyplace else."

"D'you want me to bring it up?" I nodded again. "On the other hand"—she looked at me—"he might be less shy if Wade and I left, and it was just the two of you. That could be here, or the two of you could go someplace. . . ."

Her first choice, I could see, was to be alone with Wade. "You guys can go," I said.

"No, it's okay. I'll see what I can do," she said.

When Max and Wade came back, she went over to Wade and took his hand. I saw Max notice. He looked quickly at me, then looked away. "So," I asked him, "do you think their project's going to work?"

"Why not?" He met my eyes, but only for an instant.

The mouse plane might fly. This match clearly wouldn't. Even Maple saw it. "Well," she said, "I guess Wade and I are going to head out." She looked at Max. "We're going down to the three-dollar movie, see what's playing. Max, Joy's going to come with us, so if you want . . ."

I held my breath.

"That's okay," said Max. "I really just stopped over to say hi."

"That's cool," I said. "I actually have things to do."

"Yeah"—he pointed himself toward the door—"I should probably go home. It was great meeting you all. See you in school Monday." And he was gone.

Maple looked at me. She and Wade were still holding hands. He seemed as if he couldn't wait to be alone with her either. "You guys go ahead," I told them. They protested, but only briefly.

"They left?" Uncle Max said, when he came out afterward. He looked around as if Max must have been hiding under the furniture. "All of them?" I nodded. "What happened? Why?"

"I guess he didn't like me," I said.

"That's preposterous!" he said. He looked almost as upset as I was.

Chapter 10

"He really hasn't turned up yet?" Uncle Max asked the whole next week. "You haven't seen Young Max at all?" I hadn't, though I'd been scanning the schoolyard and the halls.

"Give it time," he assured me. "It's a big school."

But Max clearly wasn't looking for me.

"Well, if this boy's so easily discouraged," Uncle Max decided finally, "he's no match for you. There are plenty of fish in the sea, and more names on your match list. Maybe you'll meet someone at the mixer."

I said I didn't think I was going to the mixer.

He looked up from his newspaper. "Why not? You said you were."

"Maple doesn't really want to go anymore," I said.

"What happened? She's too busy with the raincoat fella?" I nodded. "They're an item, eh?"

"Oh, yeah." She'd been spending almost all her time with him, meeting him as soon as we got to school and between classes, walking with him to his job. I didn't have to come straight home anymore. Mom had decided Uncle Max was in good enough shape to be by himself. But I felt a little funny, tagging along with them every day, and I knew they wouldn't want to tag along with me to some dumb mixer on the one afternoon Wade had free.

Uncle Max came over to the table, where I was flipping through the latest pile of clothing catalogs. "You know," he said, "it wouldn't hurt for you to get out of that closet for a change and socialize."

"I know," I said. "I will." I was still carrying around the match list. I could have met somebody named Andre, who'd looked okay, if I'd had the nerve to go up to him when Wade pointed him out to me in the hall.

Uncle Max took my hand. "Since when do you bite your nails?"

"I don't bite them," I said, looking down at my pathetic little stubs. "I just sort of neaten them up."

"Yeah, well," he said, "they're getting neater and neater."

He went back to his reading, but a minute later he said, "You know, if I knew any of the modern dances, I'd take you to that mixer myself."

That was a scary thought. "Don't worry about it," I said. "I'm not going, and it's fine."

"You never know," he said. "You could change your mind."

"Unlikely," I said.

"You're as stubborn as I am," he said. "And that's not a compliment."

Just when I thought the subject was dead, he looked up again. "What about new match prospects?"

"Uncle Max, forget the Match Quiz," I said. "I came, I saw, I bombed out." We were doing a whole Julius Caesar thing in English class. "It's been almost two weeks. Anything that was going to happen has already happened."

Unfortunately, that didn't turn out to be true.

It was the afternoon of the mixer when the doorbell rang. "Joy, could you get that?" Uncle Max called. He was closer to the door, which should have raised my suspicions.

When I opened it, I saw a tall boy on Rollerblades. A tall, pale, slightly pear-shaped boy with a long nose, that sort of very short, pale, see-through hair and eyelashes, and a nervous, eager smile. "Are you Joy?" he said. He was staring at me. I nodded. "Sorry I'm late."

"Late?" I said. "Excuse me?" He looked like a mouse. A large white mouse on wheels.

"I'm Leland?" He blinked nervously. "We have a date?"

My heart sank. There was a Leland on my match list—a junior, Leland Groobert. "Uncle Max!" I called.

"Is there some mistake?" Leland asked.

"No mistake!" Uncle Max came up beside me and shook Leland's hand. "You're right on time. Come on in!" he said. Leland pointed to his Rollerblades, but Uncle Max waved that away. "I apologize, Leland. We just seem to have our signals crossed." He shot me a shut-up-Joy look. "I just forgot to tell Joy today was the day you were coming. Come in and have a seat. Joy, show Leland to the living room." He followed as Leland clumped carefully across the carpet, which I realized now was newly vacuumed and bone-free. At least this time Sarge was nowhere to be seen. "Sit down, Leland, take a load off!" he said.

"Actually, do you mind if I take off my skates?" Leland sat down at the dining table, which was against the windows, leaned over, and began undoing the laces. "You don't happen to have an Allen wrench, by any chance?" he asked. "I hit a bump on the way over. I've got a problem with the wheel."

I had no idea what an Allen wrench was, but I jumped up. "I'll go look," I said. I gave Uncle Max a meaningful look. "Why don't you come help me?"

"Sit down, Joy, relax." Uncle Max ignored my look. "We don't need to do it right this minute, do we, Leland?"

"It's fine." Leland was not only staring at me now, he was smiling again. Smiling as if this was a job interview, or a personality contest, or somebody had told him to say Cheese. The way he was sitting in front of the windows, his ears, which were large and delicate, were backlit, so that the late afternoon sun shone through them. They glowed, red and almost translucent.

There was a whining and scratching and loud thumps from down the hall. Leland looked in the direction of the sound. Nathan, who'd been making horny hound jokes all week, was in our room with Ben, doing something raucous with the guitar and drums. I prayed he wouldn't hear Sarge and come out to see what was going on. "The dog," I said. "Any minute now, a crazed terrier's going to come hurtling out and start humping you."

Leland stiffened.

"No, he won't," said Uncle Max. "I closed my door tight. So." He addressed Leland. "After I talked to you, I was remembering, I had a customer at the store, a Dr. Groobert, an eye doctor . . ."

"Really?" said Leland. "That's so weird. That must have been my grandfather. He was an eye doctor."

"It's not weird at all," said Uncle Max. "Sooner or later, everyone goes to Nathan's for their shoes, and it's not that common a name. Gruber, yes, but not Groo-*bert*. That's why I figured . . ." Leland nodded a few too many times. He was still staring at me. I was staring at his ears. You could almost see through them. "What was his first name? Harry?" Uncle Max was saying. "Something like that. This goes back a few years. The shoes I remember better than the names . . ."

I don't know how long this conversation went on. I stopped listening. I was already turning this into a story to tell Maple. "I wonder if the ears glow in the dark, too," I'd say. "He was no match for me, but we could fix him up with Ludwig, or Kurt Cobain. And, mousiness aside, unless it was Hubert Groobert, is there a less boyfriendlike name than Leland? I mean, think about it: *I love Leland* in a big heart on my binder? *LELAND* tattooed on my bicep? *Joy and Leland 4ever* scratched into the stall door in the Girls Room?" I could already hear us laughing.

That didn't mean, though, that I wasn't really annoyed at Uncle Max for perpetrating this. Not only did it look as if Leland liked me, he and Leland were hitting it off way too well. "Uh, about that wrench," I said. "Uncle Max, think you could help me now?" I gave him yet another meaningful look and signaled with my head toward the kitchen.

"Okay, don't kill me!" he said as soon as he had closed the kitchen door behind us. "So he's not Mr. Right, but he seems like a nice kid."

"That's not the point." I had a horrible thought. "Please tell me *you* didn't call *him!*"

He looked deeply insulted. "Would I do that?"

"I don't know," I said.

"No! He called, and I figured, the name Groobert, he's probably at least respectable, and you've been so discouraged, and I thought"—to his credit, he looked a little sheepish now—"since today was the mixer, if he happened to be nice, and you two happened to like each other—"

"Oy!" I groaned and rolled my eyes.

"He does like you, you know. I saw the way he was looking at you."

"Yeah," I said, "like the way Sarge looks at his dog yummy."

"You could at least make a little effort to be nice to him, after he came all the way over here. You haven't said a word to him." I rolled my eyes again. "Okay. Okay," he said. "My intentions were good."

"I know!" I said. That's what made the whole thing so infuriating.

"You have to understand," he said. "My whole life, I see a problem, I look for a solution. It's just my nature. I'm what they call a facilitator. For forty-three years I managed a business. I'm used to being the guy who makes things happen."

"So now what?" I said.

"What do you mean?"

"How do we get him out of here?"

"He just got here," he said.

"You could tell him I died looking for the wrench," I suggested. "I could fall down on the ground and pretend to have a heart attack, or clutch my stomach and say I ate a bad clam. We could set off the smoke alarm. I could say, 'I've got two lovely mice I'd like you to meet' or—"

"No, no!" he said before I could come up with any more ridiculous ideas. "I got you into this. If you insist, I'll get you out of it."

"How?" I asked.

He made a face. "I don't know yet."

"There's always Sarge," I said.

Leland had one of his skates on his lap when we went back, and was studying the way the wheels spun. "Uh, sorry we took so long," I said. "After all that, we don't seem to have a wrench."

"That's okay," he said. "The wheel actually seems good enough to get me home."

"You're going home?" asked Uncle Max a bit too eagerly.

"Well, not now," Leland said, then looked at me. I hate to think what my face looked like. "I mean, unless . . ." He started blinking again. I didn't say anything.

There was a huge silence. Nathan and Ben had stopped playing. Sarge had stopped throwing himself against the door. Finally, Uncle Max went over to Leland. "So, Leland," he said. "I'm afraid I owe you an apology."

Leland stopped smiling. "What do you mean?"

"How should I put this?" Uncle Max looked over at me. You're really going to make me do this? he seemed to be asking. I nodded. He sighed. "Well," he said, "I guess you could say I stuck my big nose in where it didn't belong. I told you Joy didn't know you were coming today, right?"

Leland looked from Uncle Max to me to Uncle Max again.

"Actually, she didn't know you were coming at all. I don't know what I was thinking," he said. "Yes, I do. I was thinking you sounded like a nice guy, which, in fact, you are, and I thought, who knows, maybe they won't hold it against me. They may even thank me. But it turns out it got things off on the wrong foot. Which, for a shoe salesman"—he gave Leland a rueful smile—"is the kiss of death. Anyway, the way we stand now, Joy informs me, is she's so fed up with me, she can't really approach this date with an open mind. Which is no reflection on you whatsoever." He looked at me. "Is that a fair statement, Joy?"

The word *date* made me flinch, but I was feeling

worse and worse for Leland, who'd put his skates back on and was lacing them up as fast as he could. "None whatsoever," I said. "I'm sorry you came all the way over here."

"She was already out of sorts before. Now"—Uncle Max wrinkled his nose and shook his head—"believe me, you wouldn't want to be with her." I was impressed with how diplomatic he was being, even if he was making me sound like a major wretch. "Can I get you a cold drink before you go?" he asked. "I make a mean egg cream."

"No, that's okay," Leland said, getting to his feet. "I'll go get my wheel fixed."

"You're a good sport, Leland." Uncle Max patted him on the shoulder. "Don't hold this against her permanently," he said. "She's a great kid, and I'm sure you two will meet again under better circumstances. Maybe you'll even meet up Monday"—he looked at us hopefully—"and laugh about what an interfering old son of a gun I am."

Chapter 11

"It's probably best if you don't mention this to anyone," he said, after we'd hashed the whole thing out when Leland left and he'd promised the words Match Quiz would never cross his lips again. He needn't have worried. One, he made it too hard to stay angry at him. Two, the last thing I'd have done was to tell Mom or Dad. They didn't need anything to raise their annoyance level.

Partly it was that Uncle Max had been on an organizing rampage. That's what Dad called it, though in my house pretty much any organizing is a rampage. Uncle Max called it straightening up. And he never did it quietly. "No wonder you're always rushing around like a chicken with its head cut off," he'd say to Mom, or Sarge, or whoever happened to be around. "It's because you can't find anything. If you put things away systematically, and occasionally, when you didn't need something, you threw it away...." He began with the kitchen drawers, proceeded to the cabinets he could reach without climbing on a chair, and then took on the pantry. Dad had warned him about throwing stuff away when we weren't there. "But that's when I have all the time on my hands," Uncle Max had argued. "I tidy up from breakfast, I do the puzzle, I go down for the mail. It's not exactly a full-time job."

"So go out for a little walk," Dad suggested. "There's no reason you have to stay in the apartment all the time anymore."

"I know," he said. "I will. Soon."

Mom looked up from her reading. "He doesn't have to if he's not comfortable," she said. "We'll go some-where with you next weekend, Max. Dinner or a movie. It's just that we're all so busy during the week. I'm so behind on schoolwork. . . . Marty's been working so late. . . ."

"Ilene, do you hear me complaining?" he said.

"You better put those dishes in the way he wants," Mom warned me that night as we scraped the last of our spaghetti into the garbage. We seemed to be alternating, these past few weeks, between canned salt-free spaghetti sauce, no-salt tuna fish, and takeout Chinese. "Other-wise, you know, tomorrow we're either going to hear how he reloaded the whole dishwasher, or how he reran it because nothing got clean." She finished off her wine and poured more in her glass. "If he tells me one more time that spoons go in bowl-down . . ."

"Why doesn't somebody say something, then?" I said. "Tell him our way works fine. I'll tell him." After this afternoon, I figured I was entitled.

She shook her head. "Don't say anything. He'll just get offended again, like with the toothbrushes."

"Toothbrushes?"

"You didn't notice your toothbrush tasted like Clorox?" I hadn't. "You're lucky. Dad thought he was being poisoned. But when I asked him, very gently, not to do it, he said that was how his mother did it, and how Clorox and Lysol keep you from getting colds, and how he was just trying to help. You know that speech."

"Unfortunately!" I was tempted to tell her then about Leland.

"It's easier just to let him do his thing and rinse your toothbrush before you put it in your mouth, and try not to get annoyed."

"Except it's not working," I said.

"He stopped doing it," she said.

"Yeah, but you're annoyed all the time," I said.

She sighed and took a big drink of wine. "Not all the time," she said.

I knew exactly why Uncle Max drove them nuts. What I didn't get was why Nathan didn't bother them.

They didn't mind his drumming on the table and his twiddling. They thought the video-game noises he made were clever and adorable, and encouraged him to twang away on the guitar. They thought it was great that Ben Zuwadski was over almost every afternoon, making it truly impossible for me to be in the bedroom. They didn't believe me when I said I thought Nathan was going through my things. They didn't even do anything when, the next weekend, I caught him and Ben using my good drawing pencils.

"They're mine, Nathan," I told him again after Ben went home. "*Mine* means you don't touch unless you ask."

"I didn't do anything to them," Nathan said in his best I'm-just-an-innocent-little-kid manner. "I borrowed them for one minute. I just needed some interesting colors for my science poster."

"They were brand-new pencils," I said. "I never even used them."

"Come on, Joy," Mom said. I'd made the mistake of yelling at him in front of them. "We've got enough problems. I'm counting on you and Nathan to get along. It's not like he destroyed any of them. All you have to do is sharpen them and they'll be good as new."

"That's not the point," I said.

"No pun intended," Dad chimed in.

"Yuk, yuk," I said. Then I went in and moved the

Kestrel notebooks to a new hiding place under the bed. They were harder to get to, but I wasn't feeling much like drawing these days. I'd pull out the notebooks and put them back again.

Instead, thanks to Uncle Max's organizing, I was baking. He'd found an old set of pastry squirter tubes among the rubble in the kitchen drawers. "See, these I'd keep," he'd said. "They make beautiful birthday cakes. Mother used to make magnificent decorations."

It was the word *decoration* that got me going. I'd baked a lot with Maple, pre-Wade—chocolate-chip cookies, mostly, or cake mixes with canned frosting. But we'd never tried anything artistic. The next day, I stopped off for butter and vanilla and baking chocolate, and powdered sugar, and food coloring for the icing. My first attempt was not a thing of beauty, but the cake tasted fine and no one seemed to mind that the flowers were sort of puce and the icing navy blue. The next day my flowers came out olive green, but I turned them into leaves and cut carrot curls for the flower petals. After that, anything colorful in the fridge became decorating material: chocolate and nuts, of course, but also radish slivers, bits of pepper, anything but raisins. I didn't want shriveled things on my creations.

Cooking I did only because Mom needed me to, but I really got into baking. Cakes were the most fun because you could do whole pictures on them, but I also tried people cookies with multicolored icing outfits, and animal cookies and flower cookies. It gave me something to do at home that wasn't in the closet. It gave me a feeling of accomplishment. It gave me cake.

"Joy, it's gorgeous and delicious, but have you ever heard of too much of a good thing?" Uncle Max said after a few weeks of this. "We're going to blow up like balloons."

I brought cake to Joe, the doorman. Dad took cookies to the office. Mom brought stuff to school to share with the other teachers. Nathan and Ben stopped saying hello to me when they got home. Instead it was, "Making anything today?" It was the one thing Nathan said that didn't drive me up the wall.

They seemed to have given up on the mouse-powered plane project. Instead, they'd used Nathan's big old cardboard brick blocks to wall off this oval track, in which they'd arranged hurdles made of little trucks and action figures. I kept hearing him muttering to my parents about data, but it seemed clear to me that they were playing. "Is this supposed to be a science project, or are they just torturing the poor mice?" I asked Mom.

"He's not hurting the mice," Mom said. "The mice like the exercise. It's fun to see those old toys put to creative new uses."

They'd found a creative new use for his old stuffed animals, too. One afternoon, when I stepped into the room to change my shirt after getting batter down the front, I got pegged with a giraffe. The boys were crouched behind block barricades, each with a pile of teddy bears and rabbits. "Phlegm!" yelled Nathan as he chucked a monkey at Ben.

"Globule!" screamed Ben as he got Nathan in the ear with a raccoon.

"Groin!" shrieked Nathan as he heaved a large stuffed whale. They were giggling so hard they could hardly stand up.

"That didn't hurt!" Nathan protested when I yelled at them. "I didn't do it on purpose. I was aiming at Ben."

"Upchuck!" shouted Ben.

"Shut up!" I grabbed the giraffe by one floppy leg and swung it at Nathan's head.

"Watch it!" Nathan shouted back. "You'll hurt Giraffy!"

"I'll hurt you," I yelled, whapping him again.

"What's going on?" Uncle Max appeared in the doorway.

"Don't I have a right to go into my own room," I said, "without getting attacked?"

"It wasn't an attack," Nathan said. "It had nothing to do with you. You just stepped into the line of fire."

"Plus they were yelling disgusting stuff," I said.

They started cracking up again. "It's a vocabulary contest," explained Ben.

"I don't want to know about it," said Uncle Max. "Joy, do you need me to kick them out of here?"

"No," I said. "This room is the last place I want to be."

He scowled. "Okay, then. But I need you boys to behave yourselves. No rowdy stuff."

They said they understood. But when I went in again an hour later, they'd removed all the books that I'd piled on top of the bookcases to keep Nathan from sitting up there, so that they could throw stuff across the top. Nathan was on his side and Ben was on mine with a whole arsenal of animals. My floor was strewn with action figures, which was bad enough. But my underwear drawer was open, with underpants sticking out. "Nathan!" I shouted. They'd been rooting through my underpants.

Ben immediately rushed over and began picking up GI Joes and Power Rangers. "We didn't take anything, honest!" he said, his face turning red. "We were just looking for more ammo."

"Ammo?" I yelled. "That's it! You die, Nathan! I can't live like this!"

"You're the one who came in," he said. "You knew we were having an animal war. And I didn't touch your smelly underwear."

"Yeah, panties don't throw as well as socks, right?" Ben said, giggling.

★

Maple laughed, too, when I told her the next morning. "It's puberty!" she said, giving me a knowing smirk.

I groaned. "Don't even joke about it."

"What makes you think I'm joking?" she said.

"Because it's too hideous to think about, sharing a room with Nathan *and* his hormones!"

I opened the aluminum-foil packet of black-and-white cow cookies I'd made yesterday and held it out to her. I'd made the pattern from shirt cardboard. They were extremely cute. I was really proud of them.

"Uh-uh." She waved them away and shook her head. "Maybe he's got cake poisoning," she said. "If you're lucky, it's just sugar."

I didn't like the way she said that. "What are you saying?"

"Nothing. Just, you're into this whole baked goods thing. I thought you were so worried about being roly-poly."

"I'm not doing it to eat it," I told her. Unfortunately, I happened to be eating one when I said that. "I like to bake. What's wrong with that? I'm giving most of it away."

"Not to me!" she said. "I've given up fat and sugar."

I looked at her. "Since when?"

"A few days."

"Just 'cause of that dumb crack Wade made?" He'd

pointed out some girl in the cafeteria who he said was "porking up."

"No. Not just because of that." She looked at me. "You know, Joy," she said, "you're pretty grouchy lately."

"No, I'm not!" I said.

But if I was, I wasn't the only one. Except for Nathan, there weren't a whole lot of smiles at my house. Though Dad thought it was pretty amusing when, a few days after this, Uncle Max got locked out in the hall in his pajamas.

Luckily, he locked himself out first thing in the morning, not when everyone was gone. He was always up by five, so he had plenty of time to putter before there was anyone to cramp his style. That morning, he'd bundled up the magazines and newspapers to leave out by the service elevator. "I was knocking and knocking," he said when we finally let him in a little after seven. "Banging so hard I almost broke my cane. I could have dropped dead out there. Nobody would have known."

"What happened to your faithful hound?" Dad asked him, once we'd all determined that he was okay and sat him down in the kitchen with a cup of coffee. "He could have come and waked us up."

"Fine, go ahead and laugh!" he said.

★

It's a point of pride in my family how we almost never argue. But that night, I heard angry words. They were on the couch, not looking at each other, Dad with the clicker in his hand, though the TV wasn't on, Mom staring straight ahead with that set look around her mouth. They weren't shouting, but I was in the closet, twenty feet away, and I could hear them clearly. "Oh, please, he was fine," I heard Dad say. "He was out there reading the recycled newspapers. And even you have to admit he looked pretty comical. I mean, talk about mad as a wet hen! I thought only people in books sputtered—"

"That's not fair," Mom said. "He was scared!"

"Oh, come on, Ilene," he said. "Lighten up."

"That's easy for you to say." Her voice rose. "You're not the one who has to worry."

"He plays you like a violin," he said. "He could have just gone down to the super. And whose fault is it that the damn door was locked? There's no reason for him to keep that automatic lock on. I tell him and tell him. And you know the only reason he was out there at the crack of dawn was because he was trying to smuggle something into the trash without my knowing."

Paranoid, I thought, but probably true.

"I know," Mom said, "but he's an old man—"

"He's an old, stubborn man—"

"And we're still in the adjustment period—"

"Well, this is one hell of an adjustment!" he said.

"You think it's fun for me?" she said.

I could see everyone's side of this, including Uncle Max's.

"So you're admitting it," he said. "You don't like having him here any more than I do."

There was such a long pause, I edged my chair closer to the door to make sure I hadn't missed something. Finally Mom said, "It's not about liking it. He's my only uncle, and he's still in no shape to be alone."

"Well," said Dad, "have you even talked to him about finding him one of those assisted living whatevers they're putting up all over the city? D'you want me to?"

"No." She sounded definite. And angry. "Not yet."

"Well, when?" he said.

"I don't know!" she said. "And I can't deal with this right now!"

But somebody around here had to do something. I came out and plunked myself in front of them. "So is this just the way it's going to be?" I asked. "We slowly drive one another nuts?"

Neither one of them said anything about my eavesdropping. "Talk to your mother," Dad said. "I've told her what I think. I'm just trying to go along as best I can, taking it one day at a time."

Mom didn't look at either of us. "It'll get better," she said. "It has to."

"How?" I asked.

She sighed. "I wish I knew."

And people wondered why I was grouchy.

Chapter 12

"What are you doing?" Uncle Max opened the door of the computer closet.

"Homework," I said. It was Sunday afternoon of the Columbus Day weekend. I'd hoped to do something with Maple, but she hadn't called me back. I'd already baked once this weekend. Nathan and Ben were doing mouse stuff in the bedroom, and everyone else was not only getting on one another's nerves, but fighting colds. "Trying to compare and contrast myself with Julius Caesar."

"How's it coming?"

I looked up from the almost-empty screen. "Not good."

"In that case," he said, "think Julius can wait a couple hours? You feel like escorting an old man out for some fresh air? I was just thinking you could use a change of scene."

He was right, so I didn't bother asking why he was

telling me I needed a change when he was the one who'd been cooped up for over a month. "Where do you want to go?"

He shrugged. "Maybe take a walk to the apartment, make sure everything's still okay. I haven't been back at all. While we're at it, we could pick up a few things—my foot powder, my good nail clippers, Sarge's sweater."

I closed down the computer and he put on a jacket and his hat. "Your parents aren't speaking to me again," he said, practically as soon as we were in the elevator.

"What happened?" I took a wild guess. "You threw something out again?"

"Some nosedrops, that's all. You're not supposed to use nosedrops, even if they were still good. It said so in my health newsletter."

"I didn't even know we had nosedrops," I said.

"My point to them exactly." We started down West End. "Plus your father thinks I'm nagging him about the vitamins. He's blowing his nose every thirty seconds. He looks terrible. All I said was that I take a gram a day of C and I haven't had a cold in fifteen years."

I looked at him. "That's all you said?"

"Well, he was giving me such an argument about taking pills, I suggested that maybe instead of a beer every night, he should have a big glass of Tropicana."

"I hope I don't catch it," I said. If I got sick, I wouldn't even have a private place to lie down.

"You won't," he said. "You're a toughie, just like me." He stopped for Sarge to sniff some trash on the sidewalk. "Joy, would you take that away from him?"

"Yick!" I reached into Sarge's mouth to pull out the McDonald's wrapper he was eating, then wiped my hand on my pants.

"That's the first garbage you've had in weeks, right, boy?" He reached down and gave Sarge a pat. "It's good to be out, isn't it? You and me, two old farts taking a walk." He looked over at me. "You want to know the best thing about a dog? He takes you as you are. He doesn't question, he doesn't criticize, he just says thank you for my chow, I appreciate this exercise."

We kept walking. As we got closer to the apartment, his mood picked up. By the time we reached his block, he seemed almost jaunty. "It was a good idea I had, getting us out," he said. "I forgot how nice the city is in October. I had some doubts about walking the whole way, but I'm doing okay, don't you think?" I nodded. "I think there's life left in the old boy after all."

When we reached his building, the doorman, who looked almost as old as Uncle Max, shook his hand. "Long time no see, Mr. Mitnick," he said. "Are you back?"

"I'm hoping so," Uncle Max said with the broadest smile I'd seen from him in weeks. "We'll see. I'm thinking about it. How are you, Mildred?" he asked an old lady pushing a shopping cart. "Hey there, big man," he called to a little kid sitting in a stroller. "What?" he asked me as we got in the elevator. "Is that so terrible, to want to come back to my own house? Everyone's so quick to tell me I'm not up to it."

I suddenly understood what we were doing here. He wanted to come home. Who could blame him? I'd thought more than once, these past miserable few weeks, that I should leave him in our apartment and move in here myself.

He unlocked the door. We stepped into the dim foyer and he turned on the light. When I was little I had loved coming here, because there was always a bowl of hard candies on the coffee table. I had a special hopscotch game I played on the pattern of his oriental rug. The candies were still in their cut-glass bowl, the room still cram-packed with his mother's heavy, dark, carved furniture. The dining room, across the hall, still had its purplish pink draperies, tinkly glass chandelier over the table, and high-backed maroon velvet chairs. "Hmmphh!" He shook his head. "It feels like a million years since I was last here. Look at Sarge, though. He hasn't forgotten." Sarge was trying desperately to lead us into the kitchen. "It's a nice place, isn't it?" I nodded. "You know when my parents moved here? Nineteen twenty-six. I was a little boy."

I walked over to the windows. The plants looked

like they'd been here since 1926, too. They were at least as tall as he was, some with stiff, glossy blades as long as swords, others with droopy leaves, thick, twisty trunks and little birds with real feathers perched in the branches. "I don't remember those canaries," I said. "Have they always been there?"

"They're not mine." He raised an eyebrow. "Rose Nussbaum must have put them there. She's watering the plants for me." He ran a finger over an end table, then examined it. "She must have done some cleaning, too. Poor woman must not have enough to do. It's funny, though," he said, looking around, "how shabby things seem when you've been gone awhile. You don't notice it when you're there. You get used to it, I guess, or you stop seeing it or something." He hmmphhed again. "Seven and a half rooms."

"What's the half?" I asked.

"The maid's room. That little room off the kitchen. Not that we ever had a maid. Mother dusted everything every single day. No one cleans like that anymore." He picked up one of the yellowing doilies from the back of an armchair. "You know she crocheted all these antimacassars? Who's even heard of antimacassars nowadays? They're relics of a bygone age. Like me. An old relic."

I looked at him. "You okay?" His voice, so buoyant

a minute ago, had flattened out, and he was leaning more heavily on his cane. "You need to sit?"

"Nah, I'm okay." He nodded toward Sarge, who still couldn't believe we weren't going to the kitchen. "I just wish I had his energy. I guess the walk took a lot more out of me than I thought. It's funny." He smiled, but in a way that suddenly made me sad. "I didn't know how I'd feel coming here. I miss it and I don't miss it. You people have spoiled me so, I don't know how comfortable I'd be back here all by myself."

"You wouldn't be by yourself," I said. "You'd have Sarge. Or I could live here with you."

"It was a nice idea," he said as if I hadn't said anything. "But who was I kidding? It's not the right place for me anymore. That's all there is to it. I gotta face the facts."

"No, I mean it," I said. "It could work. Think of all the room we'd have." I wondered what I was saying. My fantasies of privacy had never included Uncle Max. They sure hadn't included taking care of a seven-and-a-half-room apartment. "We could get a housekeeper."

"There's such a thing as having too much room," he said.

"They might even be glad to be rid of us," I said.

He snorted. "You're a sweet girl, Joy." He pulled himself together. "You all right in here for a few minutes while I freshen up and go collect some things?" I nodded. "You don't mind stopping off next door for a little, do you? I told Rose we might stop by and say hello."

While he was gone, I went over and looked at the silver-framed photographs on the piano. I remembered all of them: Max and his brother Nathan as babies, in what looked like girls' white dresses; his father, with a Groucho Marx mustache, posed stiffly in his wedding suit; his mother, who Dad referred to as the Old Bat, looking like she'd just smelled something nasty; my mother, looking a lot like me as she stood beside her mother, Grandma Lily; and a ton of pictures of me and my brother. It was amazing what a dork Nathan looked like even as a little baby.

"We got some family, don't we?" he said when he came out. He was carrying a shopping bag. I noticed he'd wet down his hair and changed his tie.

"You feeling better?" I asked.

"Good enough." He shrugged. "What are you gonna do? No point feeling sorry for yourself. Come on, Sarge. Let's pay a social call." As we left the apartment, he hooked his cane over the doorknob. "We'll park this here for now," he said. "Just don't let me leave without it." Then he rang the bell next door.

"Maxie!" cried Mrs. Nussbaum. "Let me look at you." She was small and round-faced with a stiff blond hairdo and glasses with large pink plastic frames. I saw Uncle Max flinch slightly at her kiss.

"You remember my niece, don't you, Rose?" he said.

Mrs. Nussbaum clapped her hands together. "I would never have recognized her! What a beauty you've turned into, Joy. But it's not surprising. You come from a good-looking family." She licked her finger, then rubbed her lipstick off Uncle Max's cheek. "You look fine, Max. They must take good care of you over at your niece's."

"Excellent," Uncle Max said. "Couldn't be better."

"And you're getting around okay?"

"I'm getting around fine," he said. "For an old coot."

"What old coot?" She picked up the end of his tie. "The tie looks very nice on you," she said. "It brings out the blue in your eyes."

"Rose gave it to me for my birthday," Uncle Max told me.

Mrs. Nussbaum led us to the living room, which was much brighter than Uncle Max's and smelled of lemon Pledge. The floors were covered with pale blue wall-to-wall carpeting. Plants the size of bushes stood on tall, Chinese-looking ceramic stands; they had not only birds but little plastic monkeys hanging from the branches.

"This is a very nice apartment," I said.

"It's the same layout as mine," Uncle Max said.

"It's too big for one person," Mrs. Nussbaum said. "I'm rattling around in here. Sit down." She nodded toward the white brocade sofa. "Tea's all set up. I just have to boil the water."

"You don't have to bother, Rose," said Uncle Max. "We can't stay long."

"You just got here," she said. "Joy, if you sit, he'll sit." I sat. He raised his eyebrows and sat down next to me. Mrs. Nussbaum beamed. "I'll be back in a jiff," she said. Sarge trotted ahead of her. "Look at how Sarge is running straight for the kitchen," she called. "He knows I always have a treat for him."

"No sweets, Rose," Uncle Max called back. "Don't give him any sweets.

"Oy!" he said, as soon as she was gone. "Now you're in for it. She's going to talk your ear off."

"It's fine," I said. He seemed to have perked up again, being out of his apartment. I had to admit, it wasn't nearly as depressing in here. Mrs. Nussbaum came back with a teapot on a silver tray, a saucer of lemon slices, and a plate of bakery cookies. "Take a cookie, Joy," she said. "Take two." They were the small, dry ones with a cherry or a dot of chocolate in the center. "You, too, Max. I got them specially for company."

Uncle Max didn't say a word when Mrs. Nussbaum slipped one cookie after another to Sarge as she filled him in on building news. The doorman was not doing his job. "If I'm in the lobby and I see a cigarette butt on the floor, I bend down and pick it up. He'll stand there and look at it all day. It won't bother him." The Greens, next door, were getting a divorce, as she'd predicted, and the hot water was still up to its old tricks. "It never fails," she said. "The minute I get the shampoo on my head, off it goes. I don't know how it knows, but it always does." I saw Uncle Max sneak a glance at his watch. "Fridays, I get my hair shampooed in the beauty parlor, even though the girl I like left on maternity, so it's the one day it doesn't matter. But does the hot water cut off Fridays? No, of course not. Fridays, there's always plenty of hot water."

Uncle Max gave me a look. He finished his tea and wiped his mouth. "Well, Rose," he said, getting to his feet, "it's almost four. We should be pushing on. We'll take a taxi this time, Joy, if you don't mind. Come on, Sarge. Let's go." Sarge didn't budge. His eyes were on the remaining cookie.

"What's the rush?" Rose Nussbaum said. "Have some more tea. There's a lamb chop defrosting. I'll take out two more. You can stay for dinner."

"Joy has to write an essay," Uncle Max said. "She's comparing herself to Julius Caesar, and I promised I'd help." He gave me a back-me-up-here-Joy look.

"I'd offer to help," Rose Nussbaum said, "but the only thing I can remember about Julius Caesar is that he fiddled while Rome burned."

"That was someone else," he said, giving me yet another look. "Another time, Rose," he said.

"You promise?" Rose said.

"I promise." He kissed her on the cheek, then she kissed me.

She stood with us until the elevator came. "Yacketa yacketa," he said as soon as we got on.

"She's nice, though," I said. "She's very nice."

"I'm not saying she's not nice," he said. As we reached the lobby, he pressed twelve again. "The cane," he said, with a self-conscious shrug. "It's ridiculous, I know, but I was waiting for her to go inside so I could pick up the cane."

"It's not ridiculous!" I said. I thought it was sweet. But it wasn't till that evening, while I was in the closet, struggling once more with Julius, that I had my revelation. Maybe revelation was overstating it. Uncle Max had said it himself, weeks ago, but I'd ignored it. The point was, I had this whole thing backward. We'd both been so focused on finding a match for me, I hadn't seen that the person who desperately needed the match was Uncle Max.

Chapter 13

I started out thinking of it as a joke, composing personal ads in my head: *ABLOG seeks LSOL (Annoying but Lovable Old Geezer seeks Long-Suffering Old Lady). Short but Cute Elderly Gent seeks Clean, Systematic Old Broad. Deafness an asset. Sense of humor a must.* But the more I thought about Rose Nussbaum, the more she seemed like the answer to our prayers. She clearly liked Uncle Max. She'd fed Sarge. She talked so much she might not notice how much he talked. But most of all, she was so nice, I could really see him being happy with her.

It got me so psyched, I knocked off the essay in half an hour. "Not that I'm a great leader or a brilliant military tactician," I wrote, "but all plans, big or small, proceed from one creative thought, and like Caesar, I have the courage and creativity to dream." Of course, I lacked the courage to read this tripe once it was printed out, but that was a whole other matter. Afterward, since everyone was asleep—Uncle Max was totally exhausted from our afternoon, and the others' colds had blossomed while we were out—I pulled my notebooks out from under the bed and did the first drawings I'd done in months.

Even in the cold light of day, my plan felt brilliant, even if my first efforts did bomb out. "Do you guys know Uncle Max's neighbor Mrs. Nussbaum?" I mentioned, I thought casually, at breakfast. They'd come in to breakfast even though by now they were all really sick. "She's really nice. Did you know she's been taking care of his apartment this entire time? She also gave him a beautiful blue tie."

"I doubt she bought it," said Uncle Max. "It probably belonged to her late husband."

"It was still really nice of her," I said. "She's a very warm person."

"Warm, yes, just not the sharpest knife in the drawer," he said.

I ignored that. "Because I was thinking," I told Mom. "It's not that wise for Uncle Max to be here with everyone sick like this. If he went back to his apartment for a day or so, I could go stay with him." Mom looked like she thought that was a great idea. "Or"—I didn't dare look at Uncle Max—"he could have Mrs. Nussbaum keep him company. I'm sure she'd come over and take care of him."

"What, are you kidding?" Uncle Max twisted up his mouth. "I'm not the one who needs taking care of right now. We've got a houseful of sick people here. My presence is needed."

Later I tried a subtler approach. I waited until Mom and Dad had shuffled back to bed and he'd settled himself with the puzzle. Then I said, "Uncle Max, aren't you supposed to have chicken soup when you're sick?"

"Of course," he said. "It's the Jewish penicillin."

Bingo! "I'm sure there's a chicken in the freezer," I said. Was this subtle? I didn't exactly have a lot of experience in the subtlety department: on the one hand, there was Uncle Max's bludgeon approach, and on the other, there were my parents, who never said anything directly. "Mrs. Nussbaum seems like a good cook. I bet she could tell us how to make a soup."

"I know how to make it," he said. "You put a chicken in a pot, you throw in an onion, and a carrot . . ." But then he looked up. I held my breath. "That's actually not the worst idea," he said. "She does seem like a good cook. God knows she was always trying to invite me in for supper. She probably makes an okay soup. It wouldn't be my mother's—"

"I can call," I said. "She's probably at home." I looked at him. "Unless you want to call."

"I'll call," he said. "Just don't let me get stuck on the phone with her." He picked up the phone. Aha!

Good sign. He knew the number. I sat down on the couch, picked up a magazine, and pretended to read. "Mmm hmmm," I heard. "Yes. Yes. It was good to see you, too. It's okay, Rose, I don't need a pencil. Bay leaf, two stalks of celery . . . I'm hanging on your every word." Then there were about twenty minutes of silence. I was prepared for him to signal me for help, but he barely even looked up. Which was another good sign. "What'd I tell you," he said when he got off. "With Rose there's no such thing as a short conversation." But he seemed definitely cheerful as we went into the kitchen. "Onion, celery, carrot, bay leaf," he repeated to himself as he tied on an apron. "I know we have bay leaves because I alphabetized all the spice jars the other day."

I unwrapped the frozen chicken and attempted to pry out the paper package with the neck and liver. "What're you doing with that big knife?" he said. "You'll cut yourself. And don't forget to wash the chicken well. The inside, too, Joy. Inside and out. There's no telling what you can pick up from chicken these days." I did everything he said without protesting.

"Excellent soup, if I do say so myself," he said when it was done.

"Told you it was a good idea," I said. But I restrained

myself all day from suggesting he call Rose to thank her. At dinner, I waited for him to tell everyone that it was Rose's recipe. I didn't even tell him that while he was in the bathroom, she had called to see how everyone was feeling. "Not too good," I told her.

"Max isn't sick, though, is he?" I heard worry in her voice.

But Uncle Max was fine. In fact, over the next three days, while Mom and Dad and Nathan only got up to go to the bathroom and for meals, he got livelier and livelier. He plied them with the soup and tea and toast while I was at school, called out for juice and cough medicine and more tissues, helped me scrounge up dinners. Sometimes, I noticed, like when he was carrying food to the table, he forgot his cane.

"I'm sorry they're so sick," he said one afternoon while I was chopping onions, "but I'll tell you, I don't mind having people to take care of for a change." He got two glasses from the cupboard, then took chocolate syrup, milk, and seltzer from the fridge. "Egg creams," he said, squirting chocolate syrup in both glasses before he asked, "You want me to make you one of these? It's before dinner, but I won't tell if you won't." He added milk, then filled both glasses with seltzer and stirred them with a long spoon. "But what about you?" he said after he'd tasted both and put another squeeze of chocolate into mine. "I notice you're around the house an awful lot these days. Where's Miss Mabel? I haven't seen her in weeks."

"Busy," I said.

"You making any other friends?"

"Yeah," I said. "I'm meeting lots of people."

"Well, where are they?" he said. "You should invite them over."

Even the thought made me nervous. "There's no one I know well enough yet," I said.

"Are any of them, you should pardon the expression, boys? Dare I ask if you've seen Leland?" He raised an eyebrow.

"In fact, yes!" I raised my eyebrow right back at him. I saw Leland at least once a day.

"Does he seem okay?"

"Far as I can tell," I said. Leland and I seemed to have an unspoken agreement to pretend we'd never met. "I don't think we ruined his life."

"Good. But no Max."

"No," I said. But that was okay. I'd finally stopped being in that awful combination of excitement and red alert.

"Well," he said. "You can't force these things. Maple lucked out with the raincoat fella, but it's better to meet people normally, in the course of your life. Know them as friends first, and then, if they happen to turn into love interests, so much the better. Though somebody once told me"—he handed me my glass—"that there's only one thing you need to know about relationships. Get in really slowly. Get out really fast!"

This seemed like my golden opportunity to bring the conversation around to him and Rose. I took a sip of egg cream, then got out the mushrooms while I thought about how to ease into it. I decided to take the long way around. "So how come you never got married, Uncle Max?"

"I don't know." He got the oil down from the pantry, sprinkled some into a pan, then dumped the onions in. "I was introduced to plenty of nice girls, but I was never much good at that sort of thing. I was always kind of shy. I know, I know," he said, reacting to my look of disbelief, "not with family. And never in a business situation." His eyes softened. "Actually, there was one girl who was crazy about me."

I stopped slicing mushrooms and looked up. "Who?"

"Selma Greenspan, her name was. She was the book-keeper at the store. We used to go dancing." He smiled slightly. "She was a sweet girl, and an excellent dancer. . . ."

"Then how come you didn't marry her?" I knew I was prying, but this was too interesting. "You didn't love her?"

"It was a million years ago. Who remembers?" His

voice trailed off. "Anyway, Mother didn't care for her. Truth to tell, she didn't care for anyone I brought home. She always thought I could do better."

"That stinks," I said. It wasn't hard picturing the Old Bat disapproving. Every picture of her I'd ever seen looked like she disapproved of everything and everyone. He shrugged. "So what happened?"

"She eventually married someone else and moved to Jersey. There were a few others after that, but by then I was over forty and to be perfectly honest, by that point, the girls who looked good to me, I didn't look so good to them."

"You still look pretty good," I said, "for an old coot."

He half laughed, half snorted. "You think?"

"Yeah. Definitely."

He glanced over at me. "You can't want to hear an old man's boring ramblings—"

"No, I do," I said. I did.

"Anyway, I was working very long hours at the store—my brother, Nathan, used to tell me I was married to the store—and then Mother got the problems with her legs, and Nathan had his own life, what with the country club and the golf, and I didn't see how she could manage. He thought I was an idiot, my brother. 'Max, hire somebody,' he used to say. 'No one's telling you to devote your life to her.' "

"But you did," I said. "This is so sad. This is a sad story, Uncle Max."

"Nah!" He shook his head. "Sad's when people die at a young age or can't make a living to support their families. It's been a full life, with loyal friends and a good family. I have no complaints. Especially not now, being here, with you." Before I could even think about what that meant, an acrid cloud filled the air. He grabbed the frying pan, then dropped it, shaking his hand. "Ooy! What a jerk! First I burn the onions, then my hand."

"You okay?" I took his hand. "Let me see it." His palm was bright red.

"I'm fine." He blew on it. "I just ruined dinner. That's what I get for gabbing instead of watching what I'm doing!"

"Hold it under cold water," I said. It was what Mom always told me. He didn't move, so I went over and turned on the tap. "Go on. You don't want to get a blister." Then I took another onion from the bag and began slicing it. "See, you didn't ruin dinner," I said, my eyes watering. "We'll just start over. No one will ever know."

"It's a good thing we're not having company tonight," he said. "We'd be in big trouble."

That's when I got my next inspiration. "You know what I was just thinking?" I said as he held his hand under the tap. "I was thinking we should invite Rose

Nussbaum over for dinner. I mean, she has been taking care of your apartment, watering the plants and all. Doesn't it seem like the right thing to do?"

Another stroke of genius: not telling him he'd enjoy it. Just that it was the Right Thing.

"Your mother's so busy," he protested. "She's been sick. She won't want to fuss." But I knew I'd gotten to him.

"She won't have to fuss," I said. "I'll do it. We'll do it together. It'll be fun. I'll bake. You'll make . . ." I looked at him.

"Meat loaf," he said. "I can make my mother's famous meat loaf with the chopped spinach and hard-boiled eggs. I've been thinking about that meat loaf." It sounded revolting, but I nodded. "A baked potato's good with it. Or mashed. That's what we usually had."

"Sounds great," I said. Today was Thursday. "How 'bout Sunday? Sunday dinner."

Mom and Dad thought Sunday dinner sounded like a fine idea. Rose, of course, accepted instantly. I would have felt guiltier about my scheming, except that it felt like something good, and I really wanted something good to happen for a change. Besides, Uncle Max was clearly having the best time he'd had since he'd arrived.

Chapter 14

"So do your parents know what's up?" Maple asked me the next morning on our way to school. "Do they know yet you're playing matchmaker?"

"Are you kidding?" I said. "I'm not telling them till I see if it's going to work."

"You're right," she said. "Why get them going? I tell my mom nothing. She's much happier."

"Yeah," I said. "And this might take awhile." I told her Uncle Max's advice about getting in really slowly. "But listen to this," I said. "He's going for a haircut today. He announced it at breakfast. It's going to be the first trip by himself farther than to the corner since he got here."

"Do bald guys need haircuts?" she asked. "I mean, he only has about thirty hairs, right?"

For somebody so smart, these days sometimes Maple didn't seem too swift. "He hasn't had a haircut since he's been with us," I said. "He's spiffing himself up for Rose. He's excited."

"Cool!" she said.

"You know what else?" I said. "He's nervous. He keeps asking stuff like will she think less of him if he uses frozen beans."

"That's so cute!" she said. "You think they'll fall in love?"

"If he even falls in like," I said, "I'll be ecstatic."

As usual, she stopped to put on lipstick and check her hair as soon as we got off the bus. "Do I look okay?" she asked, pulling up the collar of her black sweater. She'd been wearing all black for a few weeks now. It still felt strange to me seeing her without all her colors, but I said she looked fine. As we crossed the street to school, kids streamed by us, talking and laughing. She checked out their clothes. "I knew I shouldn't have worn these pants," she said. "Do I look fat?"

"No," I said, "you don't look fat." She'd been asking several times a day. "Speaking of which, I'm doing dessert for this dinner. I want to make something really pretty. You don't have to eat any, but we haven't baked in ages. You want to help?" She was looking around the courtyard. "Maple?"

"Yeah, okay," she said, still scanning.

"We can do it Saturday morning or afternoon, whichever's better. I told Uncle Max I'd take care of the shopping, too, so if you want to come along . . ."

"Sure." She checked her watch. "Do you see him? He promised he'd be early."

"Maple," I said, "did you hear what I just asked?" I was used to her getting all revved up and distracted when we got to school, but this was good stuff I was telling her now, important stuff.

"Yeah," she said, "we're shopping Saturday."

"And baking," I said.

"I know." She nudged me. "Look at that!" Kate Lee from bio class was walking by with a cigarette dangling from her lip. "Why does she think that's cool? It's so disgusting. Wade says his stepdad's teeth are brown and mottled like horses' teeth from cigarettes. Ooh, look! There's Kim." She pointed out a short boy in a long raincoat. "He and Wade are starting a band. See what he's wearing? Wade's starting a trend. Oh, did I tell you, his real dad got him a new guitar Saturday?"

"Yes," I said. "Maple, has anyone told you you're obsessed?"

She grinned. "I know. He is, too. We've discussed it." She scanned the crowd again. "Where is the miserable little worm, anyway?" She looked at me. "Joy, what's that strange look on your face?"

I tried to say it lightly. "It's called annoyed," I said.

"About?" She looked so oblivious there was no point

even telling her. For sure not now, with Wade Himself expected any second. It was good that I'd told her most of what I had to say before we'd gotten off the bus and that we'd made our plan. Because now that we were back in Wade Land, even if she tried, there was no way she could think about anything but him.

It turned out she didn't come shopping with me Saturday, because she said Wade needed her to help him pick out a suit. "He's got this wedding to go to, and his mom thinks he's going to come home with something bizarre," she told me on the phone that morning. "It was the only way he could keep her from tagging along with him."

"I can wait," I said.

"You'd better not," she said. "We're going to hit some thrift stores downtown, and if we grab some lunch afterward, it might take awhile."

"We can do it Sunday," I said. "I'm thinking about a Black Forest cake. You know, chocolate, with the cherries and whipped cream? It should be really fun."

"I don't know yet what's happening Sunday," she said. "Maybe you should just go ahead and do it without me. But call me the minute Rose leaves, okay?" she said. "I want a full report."

Rose was all smiles when she arrived Sunday night. "Ilene, would you like any help with anything?" she asked after she'd handed Dad her fur coat and kissed everyone.

"Oh, this isn't my show," said Mom, leading her to the living room, where Uncle Max had set out chopped liver with crackers, a plate of cheeses, and a bowl of peanuts. "It's Max's. He's been working all day. He did everything."

"Not everything." Uncle Max, who'd not only changed his shirt but had on Rose's tie again, gave what I'm sure he meant to be a modest nod. "Wait till you see the gorgeous cake Joy baked. I hope you like chocolate and cherries. It's got a thousand calories in every bite." The cake had taken me all Saturday afternoon. It was probably the prettiest cake I'd ever made. "And Joy's the one who made the table look so nice." I'd used our newest place mats and arranged cloth napkins inside our water glasses, the way they did in Chinese restaurants, and put a daisy in a little glass in front of every place.

"Well, then, Max," Rose asked, "what can I do?"

"Not a thing, darling," he said. "Just enjoy yourself. You're the guest of honor."

This was even better than I'd hoped. Maybe because they still didn't feel all that well, Mom and Dad and Nathan pretty much just sat there, which was fine with me, since it let Uncle Max take center stage. I could hardly believe how charming he was being—smiling, telling funny stories, complimenting Rose's sweater, spreading crackers for everyone. And he'd called her "darling"! It went on like that the entire evening. Everyone exclaimed over the salad dressing ("a little dry mustard, that's my secret, believe it or not," said Uncle Max) and asked for seconds on the meat loaf. I did spot Nathan slipping a wad of its spinach filling to Sarge under the table, but I thought it was actually kind of good.

"I had no idea you were such a good cook," Rose told Uncle Max after I'd cleared away all the dishes. "A man of our generation who can cook, do you know what a rare bird you are?"

He waved it away, but it was fun seeing him so pleased. "Well, you know," he said, "you fend for yourself as long as I have, you pick up a few skills."

"So many people's meat loaves are dry, like cardboard," she said, "but yours is nice and moist."

"I'll quote Frank Perdue," he said. "You remember him, Rose? The Perdue chicken man on TV? He said it takes a tough man to make a tender chicken. But you better stop complimenting me. It'll go to my head."

"Worse things could happen," I said, looking at the sparkle in his eyes. There was so much I still needed to know, though, like how well they really knew each other. Had they been friends for years, or did they just see each other in the elevator, or when they put out the garbage? How long had Mr. Nussbaum been dead? And what about that "darling"? But how to ask? Where did polite interest leave off and nosiness begin? I'd hoped to pick up some answers as the evening went on, but so far, there was lots of chitchat and little information.

After tea and my killer cake, which Rose pronounced "light as a feather," Mom and Dad offered to clean up the kitchen, and Nathan went to do his homework. I had homework myself, but there was no way I was going to miss this.

"Before I left, I was watching the cooking channel," Rose said as she and I settled ourselves on the couch. Uncle Max sat in his chair. Sarge stretched out at his feet. "You wouldn't believe what this Chinese fellow created with a lobster. I wrote it all down, even though I never cooked a lobster in my life. And I'd be scared to touch a cleaver. Then he made the cutest little dumplings. He says you can buy the wonton skins in the supermarket."

"My mother used to make dumplings," said Uncle Max.

"My mother, too," said Rose.

"But they were called kreplach, right?" said Uncle Max. Rose nodded. "Heavy as lead, but delicious."

"I'm going to look for those wonton skins in the Food Emporium," Rose said. "It would be fun to give them a try."

"It would." I nodded. This was great!

"I even have a brand-new wok my sister-in-law gave me that I've never used," she said. "My problem, though"—she looked at me—"is I have no one to cook these things for. There's no point making such a fancy meal for just one person. Not that I'd attempt the really hard recipes, and I'm not big on all those hot peppers they're using these days . . ."

"It's not good for you, all that hot and spicy stuff," said Uncle Max.

"But we eat Chinese food all the time," I said. "Right, Uncle Max? We order out a lot. Constantly, in fact. And it's always Chinese."

"So should I make you all a Chinese dinner?" Rose asked. "Now that you've cooked for me, I have to reciprocate. Do I dare?"

"If you cook it, I'll eat it," I said.

"I could try that sesame chicken Chef Wong cooked last week," she said. "That looked simple." I nodded. She looked at him. "What do you think, Max? Should I try my hand at a Chinese dinner?"

Yes. I focused all my telepathic powers on him. Please say yes!

Sarge snuffled in his sleep. Uncle Max reached down to scratch him behind his lampshade. "Sarge loves Chinese food," he said. "Is Sarge invited, too?"

"Of course," said Rose. "Everyone's invited."

"Well," he said, "if Joy and Sarge are coming, how can I say no?"

"That's settled, then," she said. "As soon as I can get my act together, we'll try a Chinese dinner."

This matchmaking felt too easy. Either I really was brilliant or it was an idea whose time had come. Or both. "Whenever," I said. "We have no plans, do we, Uncle Max?"

"It should be soon, though," Rose said. "It's only a little over a month before I'm off to Florida."

"Florida?" I said. "For vacation?" This wasn't good.

"For the winter," she said.

This was disastrous.

"I'm not a cold-weather person," she said. "As soon as it goes down to freezing, it's not for me. I have a little condo. I go down every year and stay till it warms up again."

This was a catastrophe.

Chapter 15

My plan was down the tubes. But there was nothing I could do then except sit there and smile and listen to them chat. And by the time she left, Uncle Max was too tired to discuss the evening. He just kissed me good-night and went to bed. I ran to call Maple. We can't let her leave! I was going to say. Not when they're so perfect for each other. She can't leave before my plan gets off the ground! But Maple wasn't home. "Where is she?" I asked her mom.

"I have no idea," her mom said. "I'm sure she's with that boy."

"Well, have her call as soon as she gets in," I said. "I don't care how late it is. Tell her to call."

At five after eleven I tried again. This time Maple answered. "Right! How'd it go?" she asked.

"You want the good news or the bad news?" I said.

"Can I put you on hold a minute?" she said. "I'm actually on the other line."

I finished reading my social studies and drew an entire flotilla of crocodiles before I got tired of holding and hung up.

The next morning, she didn't meet me at the bus. I'd rushed to be on time, even though it meant leaving while everyone was still talking about last night's dinner, but I waited twenty minutes and she still didn't come. "Where were you?" I said when I found her by her locker before first period. She had on this rumpled, rusty-looking raincoat that came down to her ankles.

"I know. Sorry." She looked flustered. "I had to go over really early and meet Wade. He had all this stuff to carry."

"I let three buses go by," I said. "I thought something bad had happened."

"I would have told you last night," she said, "but you hung up on me."

"Well, yeah, after half an hour." I'd been trying hard not to be mad. "You just put me on hold and forgot about me."

She flung out her arms and did this melodramatic slump. "You sound just like my mom. Do me a favor, Joy? Don't give me any grief today, okay? I'm getting enough from everybody else."

"Sorry!" I said, and walked away. So something must have happened. I was sorry, now, I'd snapped at her.

I'd say that when I met her after third period, and then she'd tell me what was up, and I'd tell her about the Rose thing. But she was with Wade when I saw her next. She still had the raincoat on, even though it was stifling in school, and they were gazing into each other's eyes as if they were about to part forever, instead of for one period. It felt too weird breaking into that, so I waited for her after fourth period, figuring the three of us would go to lunch, the way we always did. "So are you ready?" I asked.

She wrinkled her nose. "I may skip lunch today," she said. "Or just get a diet soda or something."

"Well, are you guys going to the lunchroom anyway?" Why did I feel as if I was begging?

"Probably not," she said. "We're supposed to be finding Kim."

What was going on here?

I was sort of hovering outside the lunchroom, trying to decide if it was harder to walk in there by myself or to go out somewhere and eat all alone, when I heard my name.

"Hey, Joy, want to eat with us?" It was Jen and Tara, the two girls I'd talked to the day that jerk Chris tried to round up all his matches. Tara was this large, sort of sixties-looking person with her hair parted in the middle and a long purple Indian-print dress. I didn't see her that much except in English class, but I always liked what she said when she raised her hand. Jen was smaller and much quieter and looked like a ballet dancer. They both seemed friendly and funny.

"Yeah, sure," I said.

Tara spent most of lunch reading out loud to us from *On the Road,* but I was so glad not to have to walk around asking people if I could sit with them, she could have read the telephone book for all I cared. When they asked me to meet them after school and go for coffee, I jumped at it. But I couldn't stop thinking about Maple. And when, as I was leaving school, I saw her walking down the steps with Wade, I told them I'd catch up with them.

"What's up?" I asked Maple. My throat was so tight my voice came out high and strange.

"I don't know." She looked at Wade.

I felt as if there were this force field around the two of them, pushing me away. "Listen, Wade," I said, "do you think maybe I could talk to Maple alone?"

"Oh, sure. Sorry." He went to stand by the wall.

"So are we having a fight or something?" I asked. In the two years we'd been best friends, we'd never fought. Unless you counted Nathan, I never fought with anybody.

"I'm not fighting," she said. "Are you?"

I didn't know what to say. Her face gave me no help, so I said, "You got a new coat, I see."

"Yeah." She nodded. "We got it Saturday."

"It's cool," I said, not because it was, but because it felt like a better direction for the conversation.

She made a face. "It'd be a lot nicer if it wasn't all wrinkled, but my mom thought it must have cooties just because we got it at a flea market, so she made me wash it. It shrank and the zip-out lining didn't, or vice versa. I probably should have taken the lining out, or not put it through the dryer. Something."

"Yeah," I said. This felt weird, but it was better than before. I was just about to apologize for the morning when I noticed her glancing over at Wade again, giving him these just-a-minute looks. And then I saw him tapping his watch.

"Uh, Maple?" he said. "I hate to rush you, but we said we'd be over there at three-thirty."

"Where're you going?" I asked.

"Kim's," she said. "We're rehearsing."

"Rehearsing?"

"The band," she said.

I was baffled. "What band? You're in a band? I thought Wade had to baby-sit."

"I told you," she said. "We started last week."

Had she told me? Why didn't I remember?

"Yeah," she said. "When you called last night, we were working on a song. He's doing the music, and I'm writing the words. I'm going to sing. But we don't have a drummer, so he's teaching me drums." She looked at Wade. "I really do have to go. We'll talk later."

"You didn't say anything to me about any of this," I said.

"I was sure I'd told you," she said.

"Well, you didn't," I said.

"Maybe you weren't listening," she said.

"What?" I was getting this tingly, panicky feeling in my chest.

"You're not exactly easy to talk to these days," she said. "You want me to listen to every detail of your life, but as soon as I try to tell you anything, you, like, glaze over. You space out, or start making those little drawings, or if we're on the phone, I can hear you typing, like you have zero interest in anything I have to say."

Was that true? "That's not true," I said. "I'm interested." I hated the way she was looking at me now, like I was just this obstacle keeping her from Wade. I looked over to see if he was listening. He was studying his fingernails. "But it's always about Wade," I said. "Wade this, Wade that. You quote him like he's the Dalai Lama, like I really need to know every precious Wade utterance—"

What was I doing? Why didn't I stop to think that if I said mean, angry things to her, she'd say mean, angry things right back to me?

"Oh, and what you say is so fascinating?" she said now. "But I listen to you, right? I listen to you every single day, every single time you complain about your brother or your uncle or how your life sucks. You know what it is?" she said. "You're just like my mother. You don't like seeing someone else happy when you're not happy. Well, it's not my fault your life's a drag. You could be meeting people, you could be going out, Joy—"

"I don't want to go out just to go out," I said. I meant that to sound strong, but it came out a humiliating whine.

"Well, I'm sorry that I met someone I liked and you didn't," she said. "And I'm sorry you're jealous, but I can't help that."

"I'm not jealous," I said. Was she right? Was that what was going on here? My head hurt from trying to think straight. So why did I keep talking? "When I said I liked your coat?" I said. "I was lying. I was just saying it to be nice." Shut up, Joy! a voice inside me warned. But even while part of me couldn't believe this was me saying these things, wished there were some rewind that would reel the words back into my mouth, another part thought, I've kept my mouth shut for so long. "It's not cool," I said. "You were cool before. I loved the way you looked before. Before, you looked like you. Now you just look like you're trying to look like Wade. There's nothing cool about turning into a Wade clone."

For a minute I wasn't sure whether she was going to hit me or cry. Then she lifted her chin, and, without looking at me, she walked to Wade.

"Another thing," I said as he put his arms around her and they walked away. "If I ever turn into one of those girls who ditches her friend the minute she has a boyfriend, I hope somebody shoots me."

Chapter 16

My eyes had already blurred up before they left. I stood there now, my head pounding, this sick, gagging feeling in my throat. I was right about the Wade stuff. The longer I stood there in the courtyard, the more right I felt. But what about what she'd said to me? Her words kept replaying in my head. And what should I do now? My first thought was to go home and tell Uncle Max. But once I told him, he'd never let it rest. Just apologize, Joy, I could hear him saying, but if I went after her now, I wasn't sure we wouldn't both say even more awful things. Walk down to Starbucks and find Jen and Tara? I couldn't pretend nothing had happened, and I didn't know them well enough to tell them what was going on.

I was still standing there when someone tapped me on the arm. I jumped. But it wasn't Maple. It was Max. "Hey," he said. "Joy!" He was in gym shorts and the purple school T-shirt, carrying a soccer ball. "Where've you been?"

"I don't know." I searched my backpack for some Kleenex. Of course I didn't have any.

"Are you okay?" He'd stopped smiling. He put the ball down and dug a tissue from his backpack, then stood there while I blew my nose. "Is this a bad time? Should I leave?"

I shook my head. "No. It's okay." The last thing I wanted was to be alone with my awful thoughts. "I'm just upset."

"Sorry," he said. "Anything I can do?"

I shook my head. "I just had a really awful fight with Maple."

"I hate fights," he said.

"I know." I blew my nose again. "I'm a mess! Sorry."

"Don't worry about it. So is your brother still working on that hamster plane?"

"They gave it up," I said.

He checked his watch. "I have practice in ten minutes. Which way you going?"

"I don't know." I started walking with him toward the park.

We walked for a block or so without saying anything. Then he said, "I see Maple's still with Wade."

"Oh, yeah!" I said. "She's madly in love."

"I know," he said. "I keep seeing them together. It's funny, I see them all the time, but I never see you."

Did that mean he'd been looking for me? Why hadn't

Maple said anything? I was right. She was oblivious to anything but Wade. "They're fused at the hip," I said, then felt myself blush purple as I realized how sexual that sounded. "I mean, they've only known each other for a month, and it's like she doesn't even exist anymore. She dresses like him, she talks like him. She worships him. She *is* him. There's no her left. It's pathetic."

"Tell me about it." His voice had a bitter edge. "I just got out of something like that."

"You?" I looked at him. "You did?"

He nodded. "Just about a month ago. This was really pathetic. I mean, talk about obsessed."

"You or her?"

"Over the summer, both of us." He didn't look at me. "Then me, mostly. And then, as soon as school started, it was like, 'Max, I think we need to start seeing other people.' That's the only reason I did that whole match thing. My friend talked me into it. I never really meant to call anybody. But I was, like, over at John's house and he started calling people and he goaded me into calling you."

"Yeah," I nodded. "That's sort of like me and Maple."

"I was still pretty messed up when I met you—living on Cheerios, playing this mix tape I made of every lonely, depressing song I own till four thirty in the morning. I was a basket case." He said all this as dryly as if he were talking about someone else. "Couldn't you tell? No, you probably just thought, this boy is totally socially inept."

"Or hates me, one."

He shook his head. "I was just thinking, get me out of here! I am going to kill John for getting me into this!"

I laughed. "How do you think I felt, with my bizarre family standing there gawking . . ."

"I know! And then there's your uncle, looking at me like, who is this dork I talked into coming over here to meet my niece?"

I felt my face reddening again. "He talked you into it? Uncle Max made you come? Oh, no! I'm sorry! I'm really sorry! This is so humiliating . . ."

"No more humiliating than getting humped by your dog!" he said.

I made a face. "The horny hound."

He laughed. "That was intense! You ever have one of those dreams where you're suddenly on stage and there's this, like, huge audience and you realize you're playing Hamlet and you didn't even know you were in a play and you totally freak . . ."

"Yeah, right." I seemed to be on auto-nod. "And then you look down and realize you're not wearing any pants—"

"Exactly!" He laughed. "It gets worse and worse. But it wasn't you. You seemed okay."

"Oh, thank you very much," I said. I noticed my headache had gone away.

By now we were at the entrance to the playing field. I could see guys in purple T-shirts kicking a ball around, hear them laughing and talking, hear the coach calling to them. Max made no move to leave. "Yeah, no," he said. "There was really nothing wrong with you."

"Wow!" I said. "This is getting better and better . . ."

"No, it's just"—he started scraping some dirt off his soccer ball—"I knew I shouldn't have let myself get talked into it. The last thing I was looking for was another person to go out with." He looked up at me. "I'm not ready to jump back into that whole romantic swamp. I don't want to be deranged like that. The only thing I want right now is to feel normal again."

"I've never felt normal in my life," I said.

"I know, but that's, like, normal abnormal. That I can handle. I'm used to that."

"Exactly," I said, thinking how smart Max was, and what a great word *deranged* was, how perfectly it described Maple, how perfectly it described a lot of things. "That's what's bothering me so much. She was so great the other way. Now I can hardly get through to her." I pushed from my mind what she'd said about me. "I mean, I can, if I want to hear about the wonderfulness of Wade. . . ."

He looked toward the field and checked his watch. "I really better go."

"I know," I said. "Me, too."

"Yo, Mike!" he called to someone running across the field. The guy waved. "That's my friend Mike." He looked at me quickly, then looked away again. "So you probably think I'm still deranged, telling you all this. I don't usually spill my guts like this . . ."

"Hey," I said. "It's not like I'm in tip-top shape myself."

"I just didn't want you to think I'm always like I was at your house that time."

"Don't worry about it," I said as he turned to go. "Sarge thought you were great."

Chapter 17

"Why so jumpy?" Uncle Max asked me that night at dinner. I'd practically knocked my chair over every time the phone rang. "You expecting a call?"

"Not really," I said, wondering if I sounded any more convincing to him than I did to myself. There was no reason to think Max would call. I knew it wasn't reasonable. And Maple could be hard-headed. On the other hand, she knew how upset I was.... I'd had a sudden, brief urge to tell Uncle Max about Max when I came home, but I'd thought better of it. I'd sort of wanted to talk to Mom, too, about the fight. But she was full of school news when she got back from class, and then Uncle Max and Dad got into one of their standard ridiculous squabbles about something neither one of them cared about, and then Nathan dropped his spaghetti in his lap.

Anyway, the first call had been a telemarketer selling call waiting, and the next was Tara, wondering what had happened to me. I held my breath while Mom picked up the next call. "Oh, hi, Rose," she said.

I'd practically forgotten about Rose all day. Nonetheless, I could barely pay atttention, even when, after they'd talked for a while, Mom handed the phone to Uncle Max. I had too much to think about tonight to worry about other people's problems, let alone play matchmaker or think about my next move. Or decide if there should even be a next move, now that Rose was leaving.

I went to bed before Nathan that night, but I couldn't sleep. Maple hadn't called, which was a bad sign. I hadn't called her either, but that was because I still hadn't worked out what to say. I wanted to make sure she understood that I'd never have exploded that way if I weren't so upset about everything at home. That I was happy about her and Wade. That I was nothing like her mom. But at the same time, another part of me was still saying, Yeah, but why should you need to explain yourself, when she was the one who . . . So, as the mice squeaked and scrabbled in their cage, I went round and round, over and over what each of us had said. I tried to switch my thoughts to Max, to keep myself from obsessing, but even when I finally did fall asleep, I had bad dreams about Maple's mother.

This is stupid, I said to myself when the alarm went off. People have had fights before. I'm going to go to the bus stop like a normal abnormal, nonderanged human being and talk to her. It was beautiful and clear that morning. Sweater weather, but not raincoat weather. I decided that if she was wearing the Wade coat, it would tell me something. But even if she was, I promised myself I'd stay cool. What I'd say I had no idea, but I'd try to stay loose, not, as Uncle Max always said, get my shorts in a knot, see what happened.

It didn't work. By the time I reached the bus stop, I was in a tizzy.

But it didn't matter, because she wasn't there. And when I did see her at her locker, she was with Wade, and she had on the raincoat. They both had on the raincoat. I was starting to loathe and detest that raincoat. But even though my hands were trembling and I felt as if I'd swallowed a balloon, I forced myself to smile. "Hey," I said.

"Hey," Wade said. His smile looked as if it felt as strained as mine.

Maple not only didn't say anything, she looked away.

For the first time I was glad we had no classes together.

I ate lunch that day with Jen and Tara. "Where's Maple?" Jen asked as soon as I put down my tray.

I made a face. "Not talking to me."

"Why?" she said. "You guys are best friends."

"I know." I gave them the short version of the fight.

"So is it that she thinks you hate her or that you hate Wade?" asked Tara.

"I don't hate her," I said. "I'm just mad at her. And I like Wade."

"Well then, what's the problem?" asked Jen.

"The usual," Tara told her. "Love's making her crazy."

I nodded. "That's exactly what Max said."

Jen looked up from her tuna salad. "Who's Max?"

I told them about Max.

"Ooh, he sounds great!" she said when I'd finished. "Do you like him?"

"Yeah." I nodded again. "He's a really cool person."

Tara's eyebrows went up. "But do you like him as in *like him* like him?"

I could feel myself blush. "I don't know yet."

"Well, if he asks you out, will you go?"

"He won't ask me out," I said. "He has this girl-friend." I told them what he'd said about his breakup. "And he doesn't want to be deranged again. He's staying out of romantic swamps. He just wants to be his usual normal abnormal self."

"He said that?" Tara asked. I nodded. "Oh, wow, I love this guy! If you don't want him, I'll take him!"

"I know," I said.

"Getting back to Maple," Jen said. "Is she the sort of person who stays mad for a long time?"

"I don't know," I said. "She's always mad at her mother, but we've never been mad at each other before."

"You might have to give it a little time," she said.

"Yeah, don't, like, follow her around," Tara said. "Let her cool down on her own."

"And in the meantime," Jen said, "you can hang with us."

That not only felt extremely nice, it made a lot of sense.

Since Maple was not an early person, the next morning I left home half an hour early. "Where're you off to?" asked Uncle Max, who was just coming back from taking Sarge for his walk. He'd been walking Sarge himself ever since our trip to Rose's.

"Just school," I said.

"Bring a jacket," he said. "It's cold. You know what I forgot to pick up when we went back to the apartment? My heavy coat. I'm going to go get it today." He clearly wanted to have a whole conversation, but I was eager to get over to the bus.

It was so early I had my choice of seats. I opened my binder, hoping to knock off the bio worksheet, but we'd only gone one stop when I heard my name. It was Max. My heart thudded. He was with a tall boy dressed like him, in a blue knitted cap, sweater, and flannel shirt. "Excuse me. 'Scuse me. I'm sorry." They pushed past an old lady and a mother with two little kids to get to me. "Hey, Joy." He smiled as he made himself a place in front of me. "You're up early."

"I didn't know you took this bus," I said. He looked glad to see me.

"I don't usually," he said. "But we have a seven thirty math review session, and J.J. lives up on Eighty-ninth—this being J.J."—J.J. saluted—"so I sometimes walk up and we take this bus across."

"Oh, yeah?" I said.

"Yeah," he said. Then, evidently, neither one of us could think of anything to say. He stood there looking friendly but awkward, till J.J. began in a pompous voice to read one of those Poetry in Motion poems that the Transit Authority posts in buses, something about the earth is my mother, and I pretended to go back to my bio. But after we got off, we all walked to school together, and we stood around making up silly variations on the poem, and it was really nice because I was laughing with them when the Raincoat Twins appeared.

"She's being really infantile, in my opinion," Tara said at lunch that day. "I mean, that's not the way you treat your best friend, right? I mean, get over it."

"That's what I think," I said. But there was no sign Maple was over it.

Thursday morning I got to the bus at exactly the same time. I took a seat and opened my book, forcing myself not to look up when the bus stopped. Just read, Joy, I told myself. There's no reason to think he'll be there.

But he was. And he was alone. My pulse quickened. "Where's J.J.?" I asked.

"He overslept," he said.

Yet Max had taken this bus anyway.

"You're going to school early again," he said.

"I know," I said.

"Do you have an early class?"

"No," I said. I debated whether I should tell him. "This sounds really immature, I know. I'm doing it so I won't see Maple. She's still not talking to me."

"That's funny," he said. "That's pretty much the same reason I'm taking this bus instead of my usual. I ran into Laura the other morning." He grimaced. "I never run into her. She goes to Dalton, so I hadn't seen her in, like, almost six weeks. . . ."

The girlfriend. So that's what he was doing here. "So how'd it go?" I asked, trying to keep my voice as dry as his. "Was it cool?"

"It was. I wasn't."

"What'd you do?"

"Threw myself at her feet and grabbed her around the legs, whimpering and moaning—"

I looked at him. "You did?"

"Well, no," he said. "But she looked at me like she thought I was about to."

"Did you want to?" What on earth made me say that?

He thought about it. "Actually, no," he said. "Which is fairly amazing. And good."

"It is good," I said.

After that, the conversation stopped dead. I tried to think of a topic that was neutral but not totally inane. But there were less than five minutes till we reached our stop, and I couldn't let it go to waste. So when I noticed the corner of a large sketch pad sticking out of his backpack, I said, "You like to draw?"

"Not very much," he said. "But I have art this semester. We have to do this portfolio, so I keep carrying the pad around with me, looking for things I can draw. I have to have something like twenty sketches by November fourth."

"I love to draw," I said. "I draw all the time."

"You're probably a lot better at it than I am," he said.

"I'm sure you're not that bad," I said.

"Well, I did okay with the first assignment," he said, "which was, like, draw an object, but that was because I picked my soccer ball. I mean, how hard can that be, right, if you're not, like, trying to do fancy shading. It's a ball. It's round. So then I did an orange and a grape-fruit. They weren't too bad. So I tried a trash can."

"That's not round," I said. A Nathan-like comment if there ever was one, but he let it pass.

"Yeah, that one didn't look so good. So then I decided I'd branch out and go for square, so I drew my computer. But now Mr. Lipkin wants us to draw people and animals. I tried my cat, but my dad said it looked like an anteater."

I laughed. "That wasn't too nice."

"Well, it sort of did."

"I thought your dad was a psychologist," I said. "Isn't he afraid he might warp your personality?"

"It's way too late," he said. "Anyway, how'd you know that?"

"Uncle Max told me." I was afraid I shouldn't have admitted that I'd remembered. But he either didn't notice or didn't mind. And then we reached our stop. "Try drawing a bird," I said as we walked up to school. "Birds may be easier than cats."

I felt weirdly cheerful by the time I left him—so cheerful I smiled at both Richard Quinn and Justin Zuwadski, and said hi to Leland, who, I was pleased to see, was with a girl who was gazing at him the same way he'd gazed at me. Tara brought me in a stack of books: *Catch-22, Cat's Cradle, Naked Lunch, Anna Karenina*. "When I'm upset, I always get under the covers and read," she said. "I recommend it." But it wasn't till she said, "It works even better with a pint of vanilla ice cream and a bag of chocolate-chunk macadamia cookies," that I realized that not only did I have no urge to climb under the covers, I hadn't baked all week. It was even getting a little easier seeing Maple in the hall. It didn't hurt quite so much every time Wade smiled as they went past and she didn't.

Chapter 18

I also finally got my first A of the year—on, of all things, that Julius Caesar essay. I laughed when I told Uncle Max. "I can't believe it," I said. "It's such a load of crap."

"Can I see?" He stuck out his lip and nodded thoughtfully as he read. Then he chuckled. "Well, young lady," he said, "you certainly have a way with words."

"Crap, right?" I said.

"Yeah, well, your prose gets a little overblown," he said. "But I admire your *chutzpah*."

I gave him a questioning look.

"If you're going to be like Julius," he said, "you gotta know the word. It means audacity, nerve, self-assurance, daring."

I made a scornful noise.

"Never mind *phtt!* You're creative and a leader. You even have the same initials: J.C."

"Too bad I didn't think of that," I said. "I could have put it in the essay. I could have said it was fate."

"Nah," he said, "you just take after me. That's why we get along so well. I've told you how we got started in the shoe business. . . ." He went into a story I'd heard many times, about how it was named Nathan's Shoes, after his brother, but how it was really his idea. When he'd finished, he patted me on the shoulder. "Here's to courage and creativity and more A's. Keep up the good work, kiddo. You're going to take high school by storm. By the way," he added, "Rose called."

I hoped that wasn't a connection—between Rose and my *chutzpah*—that it didn't mean he'd guessed my plan. Not that it mattered much, since she was leaving. And since I'd basically given up on it.

"She wants to know if we want to do that Chinese dinner Sunday."

I did my best to sound casual. "What'd you say?"

"I said we'd let her know."

Mom and Dad, it turned out, had already made plans to eat with friends, but Mom told him the rest of us should definitely go to Rose's. I thought briefly about suggesting he go by himself, but even though I'd stopped looking to Rose as our rescuer, my basic nosiness won out.

"Six thirty," Uncle Max said after he made the call. "I asked if there was anything we could bring. She said dessert."

"Great," Mom said. "Joy can bake. I really appreciate your doing this with him," she told me later. "It's good for him to get out. The more diversion he has, the better for all of us."

At lunch the next day, I told Tara and Jen about the Rose dinner, and a little about Uncle Max. He'd gone out by himself a few times that week, as well as picking up the mail and walking Sarge to the corner, but Mom was right. Life would be a lot more peaceful in the apartment if he had more to think about and more to do. Now that I wasn't playing matchmaker, an evening with Rose Nussbaum and Uncle Max didn't sound all that enticing, but, as I told Tara and Jen, at least it gave me a good reason to bake. I told them about some of my more artistic creations.

"Oh, wow," Jen said. "I love to bake, but I never tried anything like that."

"Yeah, the decorating sounds really fun," said Tara. "You want some help? We could make, like, a seven-layer cake with seven different colors of frosting. We could make two things, one for her and one for us. We can get the stuff on the way to your house."

That sounded great to me. It had been so long since

I had had anyone over. Maybe I'd even get lucky and no one would be home.

But Uncle Max was snoring quietly in his chair when we got there, and there were two backpacks and two jackets on the foyer floor, which meant Ben. We tiptoed past Uncle Max to the kitchen and closed the door, then unpacked our ingredients and got down *The Joy of Cooking*. While I mixed up three chocolate egg creams, we found recipes both for the seven-layer cake and meringues, which we thought would look really pretty in different colors. Tara rolled up her billowy sleeves. Jen took off her rings. I pulled out every bowl in the cabinet and the electric mixer and the sifter. We made up little dishes of food coloring—green, pink, purple, lavender, orange, red, and blue. Tara was right. This was really fun. We'd just about beaten the egg whites into stiff peaks when the door swung open.

"Ooh, hey, batter! Cool!" Nathan came over and swiped his finger through the bowl, while Ben looked on, clearly wondering if he had the nerve.

"Excuse me!" I yanked the bowl away. "And those are raw egg whites, by the way, Nathan!"

"*Eeooh,* gross!" he said.

"Go away," I told him, rolling my eyes at Jen and Tara.

He ignored me. "What else is there to eat? We're hungry."

Ben eyed our drinks. "Egg creams!" he said. "Let's make some egg creams!" He opened the refrigerator and began rummaging. "What happened to those pickles we had yesterday?"

"You ate them," Nathan said.

Ben opened a container of Uncle Max's cottage cheese with pineapple and sniffed. *"P.U.!"*

I turned to Jen and Tara. "I'd like you to meet my delightful brother and his charming friend, Zuwadski the Younger."

"Justin's brother?" Tara raised an eyebrow.

"Can't you tell?"

Neither boy gave any sign they'd heard us. "Can I eat this?" Ben pulled a purple box from the fridge.

"You can if you like prunes," Nathan said.

"I never had a prune," he said. "What do they taste like?"

"I actually think prunes are sort of good, in a revolting sort of way," said Tara.

"You must not have a brother," I told her. "If you talk to them or make eye contact they'll never leave."

But it was too late.

"I like plums, but I can't stand prunes," Jen said now.

"Yeah, they look evil." Nathan made a face. "Worse than raisins. I'm afraid of them." He looked down at Sarge, who was lurking by the table. "Let's see if Sarge likes them."

Jen giggled. Fatal mistake.

"Here, boy!" Nathan called. Sarge was over in a flash. "Want a yummy prune?" Sarge snapped it up.

"What are you doing?" I yelled.

"Look, he loves them!" Nathan said. By now, both Jen and Tara were laughing. "Want another?"

"Cut it out, guys!" I said as they kept feeding him. "Those are Uncle Max's prunes. Prunes are a laxative. Why do you think Uncle Max eats prunes?"

Jen looked at Sarge. "Did he eat all the pits?"

"*Duh*, I don't know," Nathan said. "Do they have pits?"

"It's okay," Ben said, looking at the box, laughing. "They're pitted prunes." He sniffed the air. "Uh-oh! How fast do they work? I smell something."

"That was you," Nathan said.

"It was not. It was Sarge."

This was getting worse and worse. "Shut up, guys!" I warned. The only thing needed to turn this into a complete zoo was for Uncle Max to come in.

And here he was. "Are you kids harassing this poor dog?" He looked really grumpy as he pushed open the door.

"I'd like you to meet Jennifer Perrino and Tara Fish," I told him before he could begin to chew us out.

"Fish?" Nathan made a guppy face. I kicked him.

"Pleased to meet you," Uncle Max said, giving Nathan a dirty look. "What's all the ruckus in here?"

"We were trying to bake a cake to bring to Rose," I said. "Before these two nitwits fed Sarge a box of prunes."

"What? And you let them?" Uncle Max looked the angriest I'd ever seen him.

Luckily, just then the phone rang. Unluckily, Tara blurted out, "Maybe that's Max."

No one here knew I'd seen Max. I didn't want anyone to know. What were the chances they would let this drop? I grabbed the phone. Thank goodness it was Uncle Max's broker, Lou. I hoped the market was doing something dramatic enough to distract him.

"I'm going to take this in the other room," Uncle Max said, still scowling. "And Nathan, you're going to take the dog out before he has an accident."

"Welcome to my happy abode!" I told Jen and Tara when, finally, we got back to our mixing. "You see now why I spend most of my life in the closet. You should see what it's like when my parents are here, too."

"It didn't bother me," Tara said, licking the scraper. "I'm an only child. I find siblings amusing." She'd already apologized a bunch of times for blowing it about Max.

"Yeah"—Jen poured green food coloring into half the egg whites—"and your uncle seems nice enough."

"We're all nice enough," I said. "Nice has never been the problem. It's just when you put us all together . . ."

Chapter 19

"Look at that cake!" Rose Nussbaum exclaimed. "You didn't make that yourself, did you, Joy? What do you call that?"

"I don't know," I said. "Rainbow cake with nest?"

We'd gotten sort of silly, baking. Most of the meringues were your basic pink and green and orange blobs, but Tara had gotten creative and formed one into this sort of little ashtray. "Oh, look," she'd said when it came out of the oven. "It's like a little dog bed. Joy, you should make a tiny Sarge to go in it."

"Out of what?" asked Jen.

"A hot dog?" I suggested.

"It's not a dog bed," Jen said. "It's a nest. Too bad we don't have any little Easter chicks. That'd be so cute!"

"We could put it on Rose's cake," I said. "I can get one of Uncle Max's canaries." Which is why I'd made Uncle Max stop off at his apartment on our way. Which

I now regretted, because it seemed to have put him in a really bad mood. I didn't know what was on his mind, but something clearly was.

"All this fuss, Rose!" he'd said as soon as we came in. She'd set the table with a white embroidered tablecloth and napkins she said came from China, and blue-and-white plates with Chinese designs. In the center was a fancy cut-glass bowl filled with grapes she said were real Chinese jade. She'd put on jade earrings and jade beads with her rose-pink pants and sweater set, her fingernails were newly polished, and she looked like she'd gotten her hair done. "You shouldn't have gone to all this bother just for the three of us."

"It's not a bother," she said, "it's a party. It's too bad everyone couldn't come." (Nathan had wangled a sleepover invitation from Ben's mother, which didn't break my heart.) "But three's enough for a good party, don't you think?"

"Everything looks really beautiful," I said. "And you look very nice, too."

She beamed. "Thank you, darling. And you could go into the cake business. What are those, begonia leaves in the nest?" I nodded. I'd pulled them off one of Uncle Max's giant plants. "Are they edible?"

"I wouldn't eat them," I said. "It's just for decoration."

She smiled at Uncle Max. "What do you think, Max?"

"About what?" he asked.

"Anything. You haven't said boo."

"Sure I have," he said.

"Don't be an old stick-in-the-mud," she said. "This is a party. A theme party. Everything Chinese except for Joy's cake and the hors d'oeuvres. Just think. If I'd known Joy was going to put a nest on the cake, I could have made Chinese bird's-nest soup. Help yourself." She pointed to the coffee table. "I brought out ginger ale, but if you'd rather have fruit juice, or a little sherry—"

"I'm not allowed to drink," Uncle Max said. "My medication, remember?"

"Oh, that's right," she said, "you told me." Uncle Max and I took seats on the white brocade couch. She sat in the matching chair across from us. Sarge positioned himself at her feet and looked at her expectantly. "See, Sarge knows it's a party," she said, giving him a pat. "He still wears that thing around his neck? It hasn't cleared up yet, that skin problem?"

"It's chronic," said Uncle Max.

"Have you tried bathing him?" she asked. "There must be some shampoo you could try. It also might improve his aroma."

"He hates having a bath," he said.

She poured us each a glass of ginger ale, then cut a

wedge of brie and put it on a Triscuit and held it out to Uncle Max, who shook his head. I'm not a big cheese person, but I took it to be polite.

"The cooking hardly takes any time at all in this meal," Rose said, "but I never did so much chopping in my life. Not that I'm complaining. I don't get enough chance to cook for people these days. Used to be I made three meals a day for a whole family, then for years it was just me and Jack. Now except for the rare occasion, it's just me. And in Florida, somehow we end up eating out a lot." She cut a hunk off what looked like a ball of cream cheese rolled in nuts and offered it to Uncle Max, who shook his head again.

"I don't know," he said. "I know everybody seems to love it, but I fail to see Florida's appeal. I mean, aside from the grapefruit and the oranges ... It's too hot, it's too muggy, there's nothing to do but play golf or shuffleboard or get skin cancer—"

"That's not what everybody does," she protested as I nibbled the parts of my cracker that were not in contact with the cheese. "There's plenty of cultural events. There are lectures every day, concerts—"

"I repeat—" Uncle Max started.

"Have you ever been there?" I said. It was a good thing I'd given up on matchmaking. This was going to be a long evening!

"Once," he said. "Forty years ago with my brother. That was enough."

He looked like he was just getting started, so I turned to Rose. "You mentioned we?"

"Oh, yes," she said. "My friend Mimi has the condo next door. You know Miriam Posner, don't you, Max? And of course the Karetskys. We've been going down together for years and years."

"Well ..." Uncle Max stood up. "To each his own, said the old woman as she kissed the cow. I'm off to the bathroom, if you ladies will excuse me for a minute."

Sarge stood up and sniffed the air above the cheese plate, then eyed what was left of my Triscuit. I lowered my hand ever so slowly, hoping Rose wouldn't notice. He eased closer. The minute he was within reach, he gobbled it.

She chuckled. "He likes people food, this dog. Can I make you another, Joy?"

I hesitated, but then said, "Okay." It felt like someone had to eat her cheese besides Sarge.

Sarge now had his nose right in her lap. "Look at this!" she said. "I'm honored. What do you think? Should I give him another?"

I shrugged. "Why not?"

"Cheese ball or brie?"

"He seems to like the brie," I said. She fixed us both

another cracker—Sarge's with a sliver of brie, mine with a great whopping slab. We both clearly wished we could trade.

"What are you doing, Rose?" Uncle Max came over to the table just as Sarge scarfed his down. "He's been here five minutes and already you're spoiling him."

She gave me a look. "He likes it."

"Of course he likes it," said Uncle Max. "Who wouldn't like nine-dollar-a-pound brie? Rose, where's your screwdriver?"

"Excuse me, Max?"

"Your screwdriver. When I went to close the bathroom door, the knob fell off."

"I know." She looked embarrassed. "It's been broken since Jack passed. When you're by yourself it doesn't matter that much if you can't close the bathroom. And the handyman is such an unpleasant person, I hate to ask. . . ."

"Who, Conklin, the sourpuss? I thought he'd retired and moved to Florida by now." Was he trying on purpose to be annoying? I gave him a dirty look. "Sorry, Rosie," he said. "Joy thinks that was uncalled for. If you get me the screwdriver, I'll fix it for you. I'll have it fixed by the time you and Joy have dinner ready."

She stood up. "Are you trying to tell us you're getting hungry?" She went and got Uncle Max a screwdriver, then led me through the swinging door into the kitchen.

I was immediately hit with the warm, vegetabley smell of bubbling soup. I looked around. Her kitchen was more cramped than ours, but a lot cleaner. The walls were papered in a yellow-and-blue chick-and-rooster pattern. Plant cuttings, their tangled roots completely filling their glass jars, were lined up on shelves across the window. The counter was covered with bowls, measuring cups, knives, and sauce bottles.

"You must have been working on this all afternoon," I said.

"It's fun," she said, picking up a plate of dumplings. "Look. Wontons. Not exactly like the restaurant, but they'll do." She tied on an apron made of the same material as the curtains, then handed me a pink-checked one with a ruffled bib and passed me a knife. "Do you think I offended him when I mentioned Sarge's odor? That dog is like a son to him."

"I wouldn't worry about it," I said. "Dad bugs him about it all the time. I'm sorry he's being such a crab."

"He's always been like that," she said. "I don't take it personally. My husband was the same way. You say yes, he says no. You say hot, he says cold. We both know there's a sweet man underneath all the *mishegoss*."

I chopped ginger and garlic while she sliced chicken.

"You're pretty good at that," she said after a few minutes. "Maybe you and I should start a catering business. We could make a fortune, especially if you do the cakes." Her eyes clouded. "I used to entertain a lot. I miss it."

"Did you ever cook for Uncle Max?" I asked as I scraped the ginger and garlic into a waiting dish.

"Oh, sure," she said. "Back in the old days, he often ate with us before the card game."

"You played cards with him?" So that was why they seemed liked such old friends.

"Not me." She sprinkled cornstarch on the shrimp. "I stayed out of their way. Jack, Sy Karetsky, and Jerry Siegel. They played pinochle here every week till Jack died, two years ago last August third. Max often came by early, since he didn't have a family. Jack used to tease him, in fact, that he either had superhuman hearing or was camped outside our door, since the minute I put the first piece of silverware on the table, he'd ring the bell."

"Just like Sarge," I said.

She laughed. "It's funny, though. Since Jack passed away, whenever I'd ask Max in for supper, he'd say he was busy. I didn't want to pry, but he didn't seem that busy to me. I'll tell you, he's much less morose since he's been with you. And physically he looks a lot better, too. You folks are clearly doing something right. He's a changed man." I kept quiet. "It can't be easy for you all, though, having him in the house. I'm sure it's gotten better, but it must have been a strain in the beginning."

It hadn't gotten better. Mom and Dad had gotten into another whole big argument just this afternoon, when Dad complained about Uncle Max taking the entire Sunday *Times* into the bathroom. It was only loyalty, and not wanting to poison Rose's mind, in the extremely unlikely event that a match could still occur, that kept me from telling her just how much of a strain it was. I guess my face gave it away, though.

"Never mind," she said. "I can imagine." She paused, listening. "Do you hear scratching at the door?"

"Go away, Sarge," I called. "There's nothing to eat yet."

He kept scratching, and then began whining.

"Oh, no!" She put down her knife. "We forgot to bring in the hors d'oeuvres! Joy, quick, run out and get the food. Max will murder me if the dog ate up all that cheese."

I went into the living room, Sarge at my heels. The plate, fortunately, was still almost full. I picked it up and was about to go back to the kitchen, but Sarge kept nudging at me, whimpering. He was clearly trying to lead me down the hall toward the bathroom. He seemed so insistent I followed him.

That's when I saw Uncle Max lying on the floor.

Chapter 20

He was breathing and his eyes were open, but he wasn't saying anything. "Rose!" I screamed "Come in here quick!" All I could think about was another stroke. "Uncle Max!" I kneeled down next to him. Sarge sniffed his face, then whined again. "Uncle Max, are you all right?"

"Oh, my God!" Rose kneeled next to me. "What happened? Is he conscious?" She felt his neck. "I'm calling nine-one-one!"

"You don't need to call nine-one-one," said Uncle Max. He sounded okay, but he wasn't moving.

I peered into his face. "Uncle Max, are you okay?"

"No need to shout." He rubbed his head. "I slipped," he said. "I'm fine. Somebody help me up."

"Don't move him!" Rose cried. "Max, don't try to move. Just stay there. Does anything hurt you? Did you hit your head?"

"My head's fine," he said. "I just bumped it a little when I fell."

"What happened?" she asked. "Was it like the other times?"

"What other times?" My voice sounded shrill.

"Did you black out?" she asked.

"I told you," he said. "I slipped. I dropped the screwdriver and when I bent over to pick it up, I lost my balance. It's nothing to get upset about." He sounded very irritable. I hoped that was a good sign.

"I'm calling Mom," I said, fishing in my pocket for the piece of paper with the number.

"You don't need to call anybody." He struggled to sit up. "You don't even need to call the super. I fixed the doorknob."

"A wise guy!" Rose said. "Just what we need!" But she looked incredibly relieved.

"Help me up, Rose. You, too, Joy."

"Is this a good idea?" she asked.

"Unless you want me to sit here all night." We each took hold of one arm, then slowly, clumsily maneuvered him to his feet. He looked kind of shaky to me, but he started walking toward the living room. "Is the dinner ready?"

"How can dinner be ready," she said, "when Joy and I have been busy pulling you up off the floor?"

"Listen to her, Sarge," he said, "still talking like it's a big emergency. There's no emergency. I fell down. I got up. It's over. So what are we waiting for?" But he only walked for a few steps before he stopped and leaned against the wall.

"Are you okay?" I asked again. His face was gray. He looked very small and old.

"My head's spinning a little," he admitted. "Maybe I'll sit down."

I raced to get a chair. He sank into it and put his head in his hands. Still shaking, I ran and called Mom, who said they'd jump right in a cab.

He'd made it to the living room by the time they arrived. I was never so glad to see anybody in my life. "What happened, Max?" Mom said as she and Dad rushed over to the couch, where Rose was trying to get him to lie down.

"How's your head?" asked Dad. "Are you still dizzy? Did you hurt anything when you fell?"

"Let's get those shoes off!" Mom said. "Did you take your pills today?"

"Yes, I took my pills," he said. "Why, when anything happens, does everyone want you to take off your shoes? I'm okay. I'm fine. I told Joy not to worry you." I have to say, though, I think he was even happier to see them than I was.

"He's a terrible patient," Rose said after she'd told them everything that happened.

"Does this surprise you?" said Dad. He poured

Uncle Max a glass of ginger ale. We were all finally starting to calm down.

"He could have been lying there a long time if it weren't for Sarge," Rose said. "He's very smart, that dog. He's the one who let us know Max was in trouble. I thought he was whining because he ate the cheese ball—"

"At least now your bathroom door closes," Uncle Max said.

Mom and Dad gave each other looks.

"Well," Rose said, "if you had to have a fall, you picked the perfect time, before I started cooking."

Uncle Max didn't smile. "It was their first time in two months going out," he said. "They haven't gone out anywhere alone since I moved in."

Rose turned to Mom. "Did you at least get your dinner? Because I could start the dinner now. The preparation's all done. The cooking only takes a minute. And the recipes say they serve eight."

After much backing-and-forthing, they finally agreed we'd have a bowl of wonton soup and cake before we left. Rose must have been really disappointed, after all the work she'd done, but she insisted she could pack the rest of the stuff up in Baggies and throw it in the freezer for us to eat another time. As for me, leaving aside all the homework I had waiting, I'd had about all the family drama I could take for one evening. So I wasn't that sorry when they decided it was time to leave.

Mom and Dad continued to fuss over Uncle Max when we got home, wanting to inspect him for damage, offering him warm milk, trying to get him to go right to bed. "I should have fallen down when I was by myself, Sarge," he complained. "That way nobody would have been upset. I would have just gotten up and gone about my business."

"Right," Dad said, "or lain there on the ground until somebody found you. Wouldn't that have been fun!"

"See, this is why I keep insisting—" Mom began.

"Joy," Uncle Max cut her off, "why is it that the only person who doesn't fuss and fret over me is you?"

Just what I needed, to be in the middle of this! I went over to check the answering machine. "Four hang-ups," I announced.

"Probably Rose," said Mom. "Just making sure we made it home."

Possible, but I'd immediately thought of Maple. It was a week now—time for one of us to make some move. She could have started to call, then lost her nerve. I could see myself doing that. I imagined myself picking up the phone now. Hey, how's it going? I'd make my voice easy and casual. Did you just call? But if she said no, or said something sarcastic . . . I couldn't deal with any more drama tonight. One of the calls could be Max, though. I wished I knew if his review sessions were over. He might be wondering if I'd be on the early bus.

Leaving Mom and Dad still arguing with Uncle Max about who, if anyone, was going to call the doctor tomorrow, I took the phone into my room. I didn't have the guts to call Max, but I called Tara. She said it wasn't her. She'd spent all evening studying for her French test. While I tossed a couple of Nathan's comics and his sock and gym shorts back onto his side and started my math, I gave her a description of my awful evening. Then I called Jen, who said she'd just gotten in. "But I was just about to call you," she said. "Did you know Maple shaved her head? I saw her on the street tonight. They're both bald now."

"Are you serious?" I said. So maybe Maple *had* called. The slightest change to her appearance had always required a major consultation. Now I really couldn't decide whether to go for the early bus and hope Max was there, or get there at the old time, and see what, if anything, developed between me and Maple.

I'd finished the math by the time I got off the phone, but it was now after eleven, later than anyone I knew dared call. I tried to concentrate on social studies, but soup with a few wontons and a piece of cake was not enough dinner. As I passed Uncle Max's room on my way back from the kitchen with a bowl of Wheat Chex, I heard, "Ilene, is that you?"

"It's just Joy," I said.

"Everything okay?" he called through the door.

"Yeah, fine. I was just hungry."

"Why don't you come in?"

He was sitting up under the covers, the brown bolster behind his pillows, reading *Newsweek*. It's funny. All these weeks, I'd never come into Uncle Max's room, even when he wasn't there. It's like, once I took my stuff out, gave up my claim on it, I didn't want to see it. With his things all around—his books, his shoes, his robe draped over the chair, his walker in the corner—not only didn't it look like my room anymore, it didn't feel like it. It even smelled different—a stuffy, woolly, foot powdery, old-man smell.

"You look terrible," he said. "Why are you still up?"

He didn't look that great either. "Homework," I said. "Hunger."

"Cheated you out of your dinner, didn't I?" he said as I stood there spooning up the cereal. "Not to mention getting you all upset. I did a great job, didn't I, getting everybody all upset?"

"It's not just you," I said. "I've got a lot on my mind."

"Good," he said. "At least I hope it's good."

I made a face.

"Well, think of it this way," he said. "Tomorrow's got to be a better day. I'll call Rose in the morning, let her know I'm fine, then I'll take a little walk, just to prove to myself I can. Now finish your cereal, give your old uncle a good-night kiss, and go to sleep."

I didn't go to sleep, though. I stayed up till after two reading *Anna Karenina*, which was such an incredibly dramatic love story it took my mind off my own dramas, family and otherwise. Till the alarm rang the next morning, and I had to decide whether to try for a possible Max or a maybe Maple.

Chapter 21

"I tried doing what you said," Max said, "drawing a bird." There was a seat next to me, but as usual, he stayed standing.

"How'd it go?" I tried to make my voice sound nonchalant.

"It flew away," he said. "But it was a pigeon, anyway."

"Right. Pigeons aren't birds," I said. "They're flying rats."

It was a pretty tired line, but he laughed as if he'd never heard it before. "What're you reading?"

I held up *Anna Karenina*.

"Any good?"

"Oh, yeah, it's great," I said. "Of course, I don't know if in your state you really want to read about somebody deranged."

"My state's not that bad," he said. "I'm doing better."

Better was good. I could deal with better. As we rode

across town, I told him about Tara and the other books she'd lent me. "I'm sure she'll let you borrow *Anna* when I'm done," I said.

"Of course he can borrow it," Tara said when we found her in the courtyard. I could see that Max met with her approval. "I pulled out some more books for you, too, last night, Joy. D'you ever read—"

I didn't hear what she said, though, because I'd spotted Maple. She was hairless, all right. She was with Kim, that boy in her band, and some other boy I didn't know. All three of them had on the skanky raincoats and all three of them were bald. I'm not sure why that made me so upset. I mean, it was *her* head, and I'd been doing so well, by the end of last week, not coming unglued when I saw her. So why was I all mad again, just because she'd shaved her hair off without telling me?

"I don't think it's that bad," Tara said. "It's a look, right? It has a certain je ne sais quoi."

"A Halloween look, maybe," I said, Halloween being only a few days away. "Like they just climbed out from under a rock!" In fact, she still looked pretty, even if the two boys looked like pinheads. Her eyes brightened as the three of us got closer.

"She's smiling," Tara whispered. "That's a definite smile. I think you should say something to her."

"Now, when she's with her people?" I said.

"Why not?" she said. "You're with *your* people."

Was that true? I glanced over at Max, to see if he flinched, or said "Who me?" or ran away, but all he said was, "You could try going over to her."

"And say what?" I asked. "Hello, you look hideous?"

"That wouldn't be my first choice," he said.

"Okay." I formed my mouth into a smile and put up my hand to wave. Maple's smile got bigger.

Tara poked me. "See!" she whispered. But as we got closer, I saw that Maple wasn't looking at me at all. She was looking right past me, toward Wade, who'd just come around the corner of the building. So I didn't say anything, and she rushed over to Wade and that was that.

As usual, I didn't see Max anymore that day after the bell rang. But I stayed up really late that night to finish *Anna Karenina*—which I loved so much, I'd have gladly read it through a second time—so that I could give it to him if he was on the bus Tuesday morning. And he was. He was there Wednesday, too. I never asked if he was still going to the review sessions. It was starting to seem normal to see him every day. My heart had stopped thoinking every time I saw him. We'd talk about what we'd read, then meet Tara and Jen in the courtyard and hang out with them and sometimes J.J. and a few other guys. Later I'd eat lunch with Jen and Tara, whom I truly liked, even if they lacked Maple's sparkle. So maybe these *were* "my people." It definitely felt as if Max and I were friends. We definitely had ourselves a routine.

It was even starting to seem normal to avoid Maple. "Or rather, normal abnormal," as I told Max.

"Hey, there's something to be said for that," he said.

Life at home was more or less back to its normal abnormal routine, too. Uncle Max had admitted to a few bruises, and his pride was still clearly hurting, but otherwise he was chugging along, still getting in everyone's way and on their nerves. Mom was nervous that he was pushing it, going out for walks after his fall, but she was pleased when he offered to take charge of Halloween. Nathan was showing even more signs of hormone activity, if loudness, dirty jokes, and general obnoxiousness level were any indication. My own life, though, had gotten interesting enough that I didn't pay much attention to all this. Thursday morning, for the first time, Max sat down next to me on the bus.

"I brought you something," he said, smiling, pulling out a well-worn book. *"Ender's Game.* Orson Scott Card. Have you read it?" I shook my head. "You have to!" he said. "It's my all-time favorite. I've read it four times."

I started it right after school. I could see why he liked it so much. I had both a math test and an English test the next day, but I stayed in the closet reading it till it was time to start dinner. I wouldn't have gotten much work done till late anyway, I told myself. It was Halloween and the computer closet was right next to the front door, and by about five, the doorbell started ringing, and Uncle Max kept calling me to come see all the little kids' costumes. "Not a whole handful, sonny," he'd say as they plunged their hands into his candy basket. "You can take one Hershey's or two of the little Snickers. Or you can have three Peanut Chews."

"Max, that's not the way it's done," Dad called from the living room. He'd come home early for a change. "You have to let them choose. That's the whole fun of Halloween."

"Yeah, but they're grabbing up all the Hershey bars and the Peanut Chews aren't selling."

"That's because they're terrible," Dad said. "Kids aren't dumb."

"What are you talking about?" said Uncle Max. "Everybody likes Peanut Chews. They were the most popular candy when I was growing up." The doorbell rang again. "Hi there, sweetheart. Who are you supposed to be, a fairy princess? Take as many Peanut Chews as you want."

At least Nathan and Ben weren't around. They'd dressed up as aliens and taken my old plastic pumpkin trick-or-treating around the building, so I got to read in the bedroom till they came back. Unfortunately, then

Ben slept over. So it was back to the closet, where at around midnight, I decided I'd better put *Ender's Game* away and start my homework.

The next morning—big surprise—I overslept. I was so late I was afraid I wouldn't see Max at all. But when I got to school, about five seconds before the bell, he was still over by the wall, even though the guys he was with had headed for the door.

"I thought maybe you O.D.'d on candy corn," he said when I went over to him.

"Peanut Chews," I said. He looked glad to see me! "Really bad. Though after about a thousand of them, you stop noticing." My pulse was racing. I'd run to catch the bus, then run again when I got off. We started walking toward the door.

"Yeah," he said. "My brother came back with a whole shopping bag of loot, but all he'd give me were the little packs of Chiclets and those nasty, squashy, stale-tasting orange peanut things—"

"You have a brother?" I said. He looked really nice today, his eyes bright, his hair very shiny.

"You didn't know that? Alex. He's ten. He's a pain, but he's okay."

"It was your fault I missed the bus," I said. "I didn't start my homework till really late, 'cause I was reading *Ender's Game.*"

"I was up late, too." He made a face. "Drawing."

"How's it going?"

"Well, I still have nineteen left to go," he said.

"What?" We were walking up the stairs now. "You said you'd done a whole bunch."

"I chucked 'em," he said. "All but the soccer ball."

"Nineteen sketches won't take that long," I said. "I could probably do that in a few hours."

He looked at me. "You're offering to do my project for me?"

"No," I said. "I'll help you, though."

We were at the second floor now. This is where I left him. His locker was on four, but he stopped walking. "When? They're due Monday."

"Whenever you want," I said.

"After school?"

"Okay," I said, my heart really thoinking now. "We'll draw in the park."

Jen, Tara, and I spent all of lunch coming up with good places in the park for Max and me to go. But by the time I finally met him in the courtyard, it was raining. It was also cold.

"Well, so much for that idea," he said as we stood there in the icy drizzle. "Now what?"

"I don't know." I looked across the street. "Draw the bagels in the bagel shop?"

"I don't even have my pencils or my pad with me," he said.

I could feel the afternoon unraveling. I couldn't let it. "We could go get mine," I said. "I have all sorts of stuff. Including some really good colored pencils."

He raised his eyebrows. "I don't want to get attacked again."

"Don't worry!" I said. "I'll just say a quick hello/good-bye to Uncle Max, grab the stuff, and leave. You'll wait in the lobby."

As we took the bus across, it began raining even harder. Sarge greeted me at the door, but the apartment seemed empty. I'd remembered, on the way up, that Nathan had something after school, but where was Uncle Max? My first thought was that he was sick or had fallen down again. I checked his room, then the kitchen. There was no sign of him. Then I saw the note: *Going out,* it said. *Back by five.* Out? I thought. Out where? If he'd said anything this morning, I'd been in too big a rush to notice. It was three forty-five now. With luck, Nathan wouldn't be home till at least five. My heart pumping, I pressed the buzzer. When the doorman answered, I said, "Would you please tell my friend to come on up?"

Chapter 22

"Uh, is this a good idea?" Max asked when he got off the elevator. I'd been waiting for him out in the hall so he wouldn't ring the doorbell and arouse Sarge.

"It's fine," I said. "Really. There's nobody home. There's lots of stuff to draw, and as long as you stay out here while I give Sarge some chow, we'll be fine." He looked doubtful. "No, really," I said. "As soon as he eats, he'll conk out on the rug." It was amazing how nervous I felt, being alone with him. When we went inside, it was even worse.

"Aah, déjà vu," he said.

Okay, Joy, I told myself. Be cool. Do not giggle. Do not act as if you're six.

"It's pretty nice of you to help me like this," he said.

"I like drawing," I said. "I draw all the time." Not cool but not disastrous.

"That's probably because you're good at it," he said.

"The thing with me, I'm just not visual. That's what my dad says, and he's right. I can never remember how things look, but I can remember what people say almost word for word."

We were still standing in the foyer. "I hope you don't remember my words," I said, "because I just make them up as I go along, and nine times out of ten, they come out wrong."

"I have this theory," he said, "that the reason I'm a hearing person and not a looking person is because I have such big ears."

A giggle escaped. "You don't have big ears."

"You haven't seen them," he said. "Trust me."

"Let me see." I reached over, my fingers spread, to push his hair aside.

"Hey!" Just for an instant, his fingers laced with mine. Then we both pulled our hands away.

I went into the living room and sat down on the couch. He sat in Uncle Max's chair.

What now? "D'you want something to eat?" I said. "We still have four bags of Peanut Chews."

"No, that's okay," he said. Then we both sort of fidgeted around until he said, "So you're an artist, huh? Do you paint, too?"

"My dad paints," I said. "Or used to. He's the artist. I mostly just draw."

"What sorts of things?"

"Whatever." I hesitated. "Birds. But I never show my stuff to anybody."

"No wonder you wanted me to draw a bird," he said. "You're a bird person."

"I am. That's right!" I said. God, I liked him!

"I just wish I knew what to draw," he said.

"Draw anything that looks good to you," I said.

"Maybe I should draw you," he said.

I had no idea if he meant that the way it came out, or if I'd even heard right, though the way he was not looking at me made me think I had. "Oh, that's a really great idea," I said. "I'll probably come out looking like your drawing of the soccer ball." But even my lame remark couldn't cut the sudden tension. "It's so weird your name is Max," I said. "I feel like I'm talking to my uncle. Maybe I should call you O.M. for Other Max."

"Oh, thanks a lot," he said. "I get to be the other Max."

"Actually we should make him O.M., for Old Max," I said. "You can be Y.M."

He made a face.

"Well, then what's your middle name?"

"It's a secret," he said.

"As big a secret as your ears?" I said.

He leaned forward. "As big a secret as your drawings."

"My drawings aren't a secret," I said. "I can show you plenty of drawings. I draw all over everything. It's just my notebooks I don't show to anyone." What was I doing telling him about the Kestrel notebooks?

"What are they, like a diary?" he asked.

"Uh-uh." I pulled my knees up and clasped my hands around them. "They're just pictures, with sort of notes or stories to go along."

"Cool." He looked impressed.

Which made me add, "Yeah, there are five of them."

"Five whole books?"

I nodded. How was it possible to feel so jittery and so comfortable at the same time?

"This is so cool," he said. "How long did that take?"

"Since I was nine."

"And no one's ever seen them?"

"I tried showing them to my parents, once, a really long time ago. Dad pretty much just wanted to give me helpful hints for improving, my quote, 'technique'. I mean, he can draw anything—portraits that look exactly like the person. He finishes a whole sketch before I've even sharpened my pencils. But he didn't get that that's not what I was trying to do. Mom said Kestrel looked cute, which was even worse."

"Kestrel?" Max asked.

It felt okay telling him. "My character. See, I went to this day camp in New Jersey or someplace, and they took us to this rescue center for injured hawks and owls, and I got to hold a real kestrel on my wrist, and I don't know, I guess I decided I liked kestrels. After that I was a kestrel person. I do these Kestrel stories."

"I don't even know what a kestrel is," he said.

"I'll show you," I said, glad of a chance to move. I jumped up and got our bird book down from the bookcase and brought it over to him. "See"—I leaned over his chair—"It's a sparrow hawk. You can't really tell from the picture how beautiful they are. See this russet on her cap and tail feathers, and this sort of slatey blue? I have pencils these exact colors. Kestrels are so cool. They can hover, like a helicopter, and they can strike a bird in midair."

He looked up at me. "So you're into vicious predators?"

I could see the tip of his ear sticking out of his hair. "I *am* a vicious predator. *Snap!*" I tweaked his ear between my thumb and index finger.

"Hey," he yelled. But then he said, "Okay, that's fair. You get to see. You told me about Kestrel." He stood up, turned to me, and pushed his ears forward, Dumbo-style. "Big, right?"

"Not particularly." I held my hair back. "See, mine aren't that much smaller. At least yours don't glow in the dark." I told him about Leland.

He laughed. "I know that guy! He does seem like

he'd have glow-in-the-dark ears. Maybe I should draw your ear," he said. "At least it won't move or fly away."

Just then, Sarge let out a small wheeze. "Maybe you should draw Sarge," I said. Sarge was over by the table, sleeping on his back with his legs splayed. "He's not about to move, and he's not nearly as self-conscious as the rest of us."

"Self-conscious? He's inert." He crouched down and scratched Sarge's blotchy gray belly. Sarge didn't move. "He's as inanimate as my soccer ball."

"He's not inanimate," I said. "He springs to life sometimes."

"Don't remind me!"

I giggled. "He runs pretty fast to his bowl, too," I said. "And he's a mighty hunter. Watch this." I kneeled down next to Max and whispered in Sarge's ear: *"Sic 'em, Sarge!"* Sarge didn't stir. "That's funny, that's supposed to get him going. *Sic 'em, Sarge!"* I said, a lot louder. Again, nothing. I gave Sarge's belly a scratch. His leg twitched. We laughed.

"He's tired." Max reached out to scratch him, too. "Had a rough day at the office." Our hands brushed. "I hate to break it to you, Joy, but this dog's hunting days are over."

"Well, anyway," I said, "when he was young, he was a world-class ratter."

"Now he's a world-class lump."

"Stop insulting this poor dog," I said. Neither one of us had moved our hands away. We continued scratching. "No, seriously. Uncle Max said the super in his building, which is who he got Sarge from, told him Sarge wiped out the entire rat population in the basement."

"Yeah, fifteen years ago." Max smelled his hand. "Phew! He doesn't smell too great." He held his hand under my nose.

I pushed it away. "No, thanks. I know what he smells like."

"Okay." He stood up. "We've put this off long enough. I'm going to wash my hands and then it's drawing time. I might start out with the coffee table."

I showed him to the kitchen. Then I went to get the art supplies. As I opened the door, I heard the mice squeaking. Which is what gave me my idea. I had to step over all Nathan's Halloween candy, sorted by kind and lined up in neat rows, but I felt a weird surge of excitement as I peeked in the cage. "Hey, Max," I called. "Max, come in here! Forget the table!" I said when he appeared. "Meet your new drawing subjects."

He sidestepped the candy and peered into the cage. "I don't think so," he said.

"Oh, come on," I said, "they're a lot cuter than pigeons." I moved the cage to the floor, then kneeled down and looked in. The mice scurried to the far corner.

"No." He squatted next to me. "One, it's too hard to see inside there. Two, if I can't draw a trash can, how am I going to draw two hyperactive mice?"

"Two," I said, "don't be so negative. And one, we'll let them out."

"Oh, that's a brilliant idea!" he said. "They'll run right under the bed."

"We're not going to let them run around the room, dummy!" I said as if this was a real plan, not something that had popped into my head that instant. "We'll put them in the racetrack."

"Oh, is that what that is?" he said, looking at the oval of cardboard brick blocks with its obstacles made of little trucks and action figures.

"Yeah," I said, "he's training them."

"For what?"

"Some sort of mousy marathon?" This idea was sounding more and more inevitable to me. I scratched the cage bars to get the mice's attention.

"They are somewhat cute," he said. "But won't he be upset?"

"Nathan?" I said. "He has nothing to complain about. He gets into my stuff all the time, and I never even set foot on his side. Plus we'll put them back before he gets home."

"Who we?" he said. "I don't like rodents."

"Did you ever touch one?"

"No. Did you?"

"No," I admitted. We were both laughing pretty hard by now. "But I bet they feel cuddly and nice. Like little stuffed animals."

"If you say so."

I opened the cage door and stuck my hand in. One mouse dived under the wood shavings. The other scuttled to the corner. I snatched him.

"Careful!" Max warned. "Don't squeeze him."

"Don't worry." I cupped my hands carefully around the mouse. He felt amazingly small and soft and fragile. I could feel his heart beating and his claws against my palm, but he didn't struggle to escape. I dropped him inside the track, then reached back into the cage, caught the second mouse, and plopped him in, too. They immediately started sniffing around the G.I. Joes. "See," I said. "They're having a great time. They're totally at home. They like it in there. Nathan and Ben put them in there every day." I stood up. "You keep an eye on them. I'll get the drawing paper."

"You're going to draw, too, right?" he said.

"Yeah, definitely." We'd left the door to the room open when Max came in. I wondered as I went by if that was wise. But being alone together in here with the door closed felt like a bit much. I got two pads and some pencils from their hiding place under my bed, then came back around and sat cross-legged next to Max and began drawing.

This was harder than I'd thought, though. For one thing, I wasn't used to drawing things that moved. But also I was way too charged up to concentrate. "How's yours going?" I asked after a few minutes.

"Well, I've got an okay drawing of Nathan's block," he said. "And right now I'm doing a bite-sized Mars bar, but unless we, like, drug these dudes to get them to stay still . . ."

"Can I see?" I leaned closer.

"No!" He covered the pad with his arms.

I was just starting to get somewhere when I heard sounds from down the hall. "Uh-oh! Max, did you hear something?"

He looked up. "No, why?"

The sounds had stopped. I checked my watch. "Oh, God! It's five twenty already!" I said. "You catch this guy. I'll grab the other." He put his pad down, got up on his knees, and leaned over. So did I. "You ready? On the count of three . . ."

My mouse scooted away, but Max caught his and cupped it between his hands. "Quick, open the cage!" he cried. But before I could get the door open for him, he'd dropped the mouse inside the track again. "*Eeooh! Yuck!*" He wiped his hand frantically against his leg.

He looked so horrified I started laughing. Then he was laughing, too, and the mice were dashing around like maniacs, and that made us laugh even harder.

That's when I glanced up and saw Sarge standing right outside the door. His head was cocked, his ears up, his eyes narrowed, staring at the freaked-out mice. "Oh, whew!" I said. "It's only Sarge! I was so sure it was Nathan. Or Uncle Max! That's all I need, for Uncle Max to walk in and find you here. He'd be quizzing me about it for—"

"Look at him," Max was laughing so hard he could hardly talk. "The mighty hunter's looking mighty goofy."

"What do you want from him?" I said. "He just woke up. Plus nobody said *sic 'em!* Am I right, Sarge? Mr. Attack Dog doesn't attack unless you say, *sic 'em!*" But before I could even blink, never mind jump up and slam the door, he did.

Chapter 23

There was no stopping him. There must have been six feet between the doorway and the blocks, but he was there before I could move. For an instant, it was still funny. He looked like a cartoon dog—his teeth bared, his jaws snapping, his head darting this way and that. But then his jaws closed inches from a frenzied mouse. It tried to wedge itself between the blocks while the other dashed crazily among the action figures. *Snap!* This time I could hear his teeth closing. Thank God for that cone around his neck! He knocked over the G.I. Joes. The mice got even more frantic. He knocked the blocks aside. Now at least they might be able to escape. But again he hunkered down and lunged forward, his head low to the ground as it could go, so the lampshade scraped the floor like a snowplow. Again his teeth closed on empty air.

"Do something!" Max cried. A mouse had gotten

scooped up in the lampshade! It raced from one side to the other, scrabbling for a foothold on the plastic, trying desperately to climb out, squeaking as Sarge flailed his head from side to side. I don't know if this went on for a second or a minute or an hour. Max unfroze before I did. He ran to Sarge and straddled him, clasping him between his knees, grabbed his collar, and then, like he was capturing an alligator, reached his hand into the front of the cone and clamped the dog's jaws shut. The mouse was still trapped inside the cone. "Joy, you going to help me out here?" he said.

But before I could rescue the mouse, Nathan was there, yelling, "Get him out of there! Hurry, Joy! He'll eat him!"

"She's trying," Max said. "Could you stop screaming?"

"What's *he* doing here?" Nathan screamed. "Where's Ludwig? Is Ludwig dead? Did Sarge kill Ludwig?"

I wanted to scream, too, but I managed to grab the mouse. Sarge growled. "Don't let go of him!" I begged Max. I dumped the mouse back in the cage and latched the door. "Okay, Sarge." I was shaking all over, but I tried to make my voice sound calm. "Hunt's over. Lie down. Be a good dog."

Amazingly, Sarge obeyed. The room was a shambles—blocks and toys strewn all around, Halloween candies everywhere—but it was over. I could breathe again. Sarge stood up meekly when I took hold of his collar, hanging his head as I led him to Uncle Max's room and shut him in.

Max was looking under the bed when I got back. I could hear Nathan sniffling as he searched through the debris. I went over to the cage, which was now back on the dresser. The mouse was scratching around like nothing had happened. "See, Nathan?" I told him. "Kurt's fine. He's already forgotten."

"Yeah, but where's Ludwig?" he said. "Ludwig isn't here. Max, do you think Sarge ate him?"

"Shut up!" I said. "Dogs don't eat mice!" I'd die if Sarge had eaten Ludwig. "He didn't eat Ludwig." My voice was shaking even more than Nathan's. "He couldn't have eaten him."

"Then where is he? I can't find him."

"Stop crying!" I said. It was five thirty. Mom would be home soon. Uncle Max was already late. This was enough of a zoo without them finding Max here. "Max, you'd better go."

"D'you have a flashlight?" he said. "I can't go till we find Ludwig."

"Just leave!" I said. "We'll find Ludwig. He's in here somewhere."

"You sure it's okay?"

"I'll call you the minute we find him," I said.

"Look, Nathan, I'm sorry. I'm really sorry," I said

once Max had gone. "We'll find Ludwig. I'll get the flashlight. I just don't want anyone to know Max was here, okay? They don't need to know."

"What was he doing here?" he said. "What were you doing with my mice?"

"Drawing, okay?" I shone the light under the bed, under the dresser, in the bookcases, into the closet, while Nathan crawled around going, "Here, mouse, here, mouse, here, Ludwig!" I was afraid to look too hard, terrified we'd find him dead. Or partly eaten. "Listen, I'll make this up to you," I said. "I'll clean the cage for the rest of their lives. I'll feed them for you. I'll do anything you want. Just don't tell them what happened. Don't say anything about Max."

There was still no sign of Ludwig. "Is he in my shoe?" Nathan asked. "They love shoes. Check my sneakers." He wasn't in the sneakers. We pulled all the old junk out of the bottom of the closet.

Somewhere in here, Mom rushed in, still carrying her grocery bags. "Where's Uncle Max?" she said. "What's going on?"

"We can't find Ludwig!" Nathan looked about to cry again.

"We had a little incident," I said. "Sarge sort of ran amok."

"He may have eaten Ludwig," Nathan said.

"Where's Uncle Max?" Mom said. "It's pouring rain. He didn't say where he was going?"

"He just left a note that he was going out," I said. "It said back at five."

"It's ten past six," she said. "I called at noon! Where could he have gone?"

"Stop saying he ate Ludwig!" I told Nathan when she left. "Just keep looking." A three-inch mouse or mouse corpse, though, in a room full of rubble?

I was almost ready to give up when Nathan shouted, "Here he is! I found him! Joy, come quick!"

Sure enough, there was Ludwig, alive and well behind the closet door and nibbling a Mars bar.

"Good Ludwig!" Nathan's face was radiant. "I knew you were a smart mouse! Look at him, Joy, he's already eaten the whole wrapper."

He'd just gotten him in the cage when Dad and Uncle Max appeared in their dripping coats, followed by Mom, looking no calmer. "What happened?" Uncle Max demanded.

"Yeah, what's going on?" Dad said.

"Sarge went berserk!" Nathan said. "He would have killed both of them! He was, like, rabid. He would have eaten them in a second."

"Something must have set him off," said Uncle Max. Please, Nathan, I prayed, don't tell them it was me!

"He was just standing there in the doorway," I said, "looking the way he always looks, you know, old and sluggish, and then, like out of nowhere . . ." Which was not strictly true, but luckily Uncle Max interrupted.

"I keep telling you," he said. "He may be old, but there's nothing sluggish about him. Once a ratter, always a ratter. It's in his genes. You can't expect him to distinguish between rats and mice. Or between pests and pets."

"Well, he's locked up now," I said. "I locked him up."

"And he's going to stay locked up," he said. "I should have locked him in my room when I went out."

"Maybe, but why was their door open?" said Dad. "I don't understand. No one's explaining to me how this happened."

"No one around here's explaining anything at all," said Mom, looking at Uncle Max.

Was this where I got busted? I looked at Nathan. Miraculously, he didn't say anything. I needed to call Max to tell him Ludwig was okay, but I couldn't risk leaving Nathan alone with them, so I stayed right by him when Mom and Dad followed Uncle Max to the living room, reminding him how I'd rescued Kurt and repeating all the things I'd do for him if he kept his mouth shut.

"What's the big deal if they know Max was here?" he said.

"No big deal," I said. "I just don't want to get Uncle Max started."

"Why? Do you love him? You do, don't you!" He waggled his eyebrows. "What were you two doing in here, anyway?"

"Shut up!" I said. What was this? How had he gone so quickly from pathetic little boy to leering Hormone Kid? I began looking for the sketch pads, which, in all the commotion, I'd forgotten. I crawled around till I found one under the bed. "See?" I held it up. "I told you. We were drawing. Max has an art project."

"Ri-i-i-ight!" he said.

I made it through dinner without the words *Max* or *sic 'em* crossing anybody's lips, but only because Mom was crying. I'd never seen Mom cry. I'd almost never even heard her raise her voice. It was awful and embarrassing. It would have been even more upsetting if my circuits weren't already so overloaded. And if I hadn't been preoccupied with this call to Max.

"I don't know what you're still so upset about," Uncle Max said, in what was clearly the continuation of an argument. "I'm a grown man, Ilene. If you're going to put out an all points bulletin every time I set foot from the house—"

"You were out all day," she said. "I only called Marty and Rose. I wouldn't have been so upset if she didn't say she hadn't seen you since three o'clock."

"Why would Rose know where I am?" he said. "I don't tell Rose my every move. Now you've gotten Rose all upset, too."

"All I want"—Mom spoke very slowly, trying to keep her voice steady—"is a quiet, peaceful life with no surprises, no fights, no emergencies, no one getting hysterical, no one falling down. I want to go to school, not have to yell at everyone all day long, take my midterms without having to worry about where everybody is, and come home and have a nice dinner."

"Before I lived with you, you never knew where I was," Uncle Max said. "You didn't worry then."

"Yes, but you weren't sick then." Her voice rose again. "You had a fall less than a week ago."

"I'm not sick now!" he said. "And would you stop with the fall!"

"Don't shout at her, Max!" said Dad, who'd stayed out of it till now. "You could have called. That's all she's saying."

"You worry when I don't go anywhere, you worry when I do!" Uncle Max's face was turning red. "I'm not your child, Ilene, I'm your uncle, who used to take care of you."

"He has a point, Ilene," Dad said. "You wanted him to be more independent and now you're freaking out about it."

"So you're on his side." Her face was red, too. "And I'm not freaking out—"

"Okay." Dad put his hands up. "Sorry, I shouldn't have put it that way. Listen, Max, I don't think you realize what a strain this all is. If you tried looking at it from our side for once—"

"What's all this side talk?" Uncle Max stood up. "I think about your side all the time!"

"Where are you going?" Mom said.

"To take a pill," he said.

"You don't feel well?" She pushed her chair back. "I'll get it."

"I feel fine," he said, "considering that I just came home to find out my dog's almost killed Nathan's pets. I have a real problem now that he knows those mice are in there. He's no dope, Sarge, much though you all love to make fun of him. He's going to remember. I'm going to have to keep him locked up in my room now, except for walks and meals."

"Nobody makes fun of him," Dad said, which was a lie, but we let it stand. "And you're not going to have to lock him up. They'll keep the door closed."

Uncle Max looked at me. "What if they forget?"

"How could we possibly forget?" I said.

"Can I be excused to eat my candy now?" Nathan said.

Dad stood up. "I think we're all going to be excused," he said. "Come on, Ilene. Go wash your face. We're going out!"

Max picked up the phone on the first ring. "Is everything okay?" he asked.

"No," I said, "but we found Ludwig. The mice are in the best shape of anyone around here. That's the good part of having a pea-sized brain." He laughed, which made me feel a little better. "My mom just had a meltdown," I said. "She and Dad had to go out and walk around, they were so upset."

"About us?" He sounded worried.

"No, about Uncle Max." I summarized the fight.

"Phew! So you're not in trouble?"

"Not yet," I said. "But it's a mess around here. And it's not getting better."

"How's Sarge?"

"Still depressed," I said. "When I went in to Uncle Max's room before dinner, he wouldn't even look at me. Though now of course Uncle Max is convinced he's a mouse murderer and says he has to keep him locked up all the time."

"Great! Has at least Nathan recovered?"

"If you want to call it that," I said.

"It was pretty bad this afternoon," he said.

It was pretty bad, but talking to him was bringing back how good it had been, before Sarge and everyone else went nuts. "You know," I said, "after all that, you never told me your middle name. I mean, I told you about my notebooks."

"You saw my ears, though," he said.

"A nonevent," I said, "whereas you pretty much saw me at my worst . . ."

"That's your worst?"

"Siccing a known ratter on my brother's pets?"

"That wasn't all you," he said. "I was right there, too."

I couldn't believe how nice he was. "So what is it," I said, "this dreaded middle name?"

"Another time," he said.

"When?"

"Well," he said, "we still have to finish the drawings. I still have seventeen to do by Monday, remember?"

Chapter 24

I didn't find out his middle name till sometime the next week, but so much else happened with him I forgot about it. We spent all Saturday afternoon drawing in Riverside Park. We didn't talk that much, just sort of walked around and drew. It was a bright, chilly day. I did two pictures I kind of liked, one a Hudson River scene, with seagulls and sailboats, the other of little kids on the jungle gym. Max drew boats, a bench, the sewage treatment plant, a lot of rocks, and his hot dogs, one of which he got with sauerkraut so he could turn lunch into two sketches. "It feels so good not to be deranged," he told me as we swung on the kiddy swings. "It's amazing how much better everything works."

"I know what you mean," I said, even though I wondered what he was saying. Was he suddenly underanged? Had this happened overnight? And, what, if anything, did this have to do with me?

The soccer season had finished, so I saw him not

only mornings on the bus but sometimes after school, too. One afternoon Jen, Tara, and I walked him to Seventy-second Street, where he was meeting J.J. Another day, he walked with us down to Jen's ballet lesson. Another time, he asked us all to help him pick out a CD for his dad's birthday.

I was standing beside him at the Oldies section in Tower Records when he suddenly said, "Hamburger."

I stopped thumbing through Disco Hits. "You're hungry?"

"No," he said, "my middle name. It was my mother's maiden name."

"That's not so terrible," I said.

"Oh, no?" he said.

"I was imagining, like, Eggbert or Marmaduke. Max Marmaduke . . ."

His eyebrows went up. "This might be worse. Big Max? Special sauce, lettuce, onions, cheese? And I was a little short kid, I mean, truly petite. . . ."

I laughed.

"It wasn't funny. Not in the fifth grade, anyway."

"Sorry!" I said. "But you know, as secrets go, yours are pretty low level."

"Yeah, well," he said, "now you know all of them."

"And you know all mine," I said.

Except for one.

"Do not encourage me," I told Jen and Tara the

next week. We were in the lunchroom. They'd been discussing whether something counted as a date if it just sort of happened.

"Of course it does," Jen had said.

"It's not like we're even alone," I'd said. "You guys are always there."

"Doesn't matter," she said. "Anyone with eyes can see that he's asking all of us because he wants to be with you. And you were alone all last Saturday."

"Yes," I said. "But it was outside. We were working. He was doing homework."

"Yeah, right," she said. "You agree with me, right, Tara? They're dating."

Tara said she lacked enough experience on the subject to give an opinion.

"Hey, none of us is exactly loaded with experience," I said. "That's the sort of thing Maple always knows. She reads it in, like, *Seventeen*." Maple happened to be sitting several tables away from us with the guys from her band. Though we were still making sure never to take the same bus, we did seem to be able to inhabit the same room, if it was big enough. I looked up to make sure she hadn't heard her name, but she and Wade were holding hands across the table, deep in some conversation. "Look at them," I said. "Derangement at its finest."

"Yeah, I guess I'm just reading the wrong things," said Tara. "Think how much cooler I could be."

"All of us," I said. "Forget Russian novels. We should be reading *Unlock Your Inner Babe*."

"I don't think I have an inner babe," Jen said.

"I definitely do," Tara said, "but there's no point letting her out for three more months. My parents won't even let me go out at night till I'm fifteen."

"Bummer," I said.

"Yeah, well, they're pretty old." She looked up from her sandwich. "By the way, what's your parents' dating policy, Joy? When he asks you for a real date, they'll let you go, right?"

"I hope," I said. But it didn't come up because he didn't, and I wasn't about to bring it up and get everybody started. So far I'd managed not to say a word about him. That wasn't difficult, since I was home a lot less now, and Mom and Dad seemed more concerned with getting along with Uncle Max than about the details of my daily life. It was more than a week since the blow-up. We were all still walking on eggshells, Uncle Max included, though he was out of the house even more. I noticed he was being very careful always to leave a note and to be back by five, but he bristled a few times at breakfast when Mom asked where he'd be going. "Where do you think?" he said. "To the betting parlor. To a peep show. To Moe's Saloon. Just out and about, Ilene. Believe me, nowhere interesting."

It was actually good that Max never called, considering all the humiliating possibilities if Uncle Max answered. Or worse, Nathan, who was still saying, "How's Max, hint, hint?" Not in front of the family, but invariably when Ben was right beside him, ready to snicker.

"Oh, do you want me to clean the mouse cage?" I'd asked the first time. Then, "Shall I change the water?" Then, "What now, sire?" After a few days of this, I'd said, "Come on, Nathan, haven't I bought you off yet?"

"No," he said. "This is great. When's he coming over again so I can blackmail you some more?"

"Do I look that crazy?" I said. "Try never."

"Come on, when's your next date?"

"We're not dating," I said. "There's no date."

That Friday afternoon, though, after we all went for ice cream—Max, Jen, Tara, J.J., and I—when the others began to drift away, Max showed no signs of leaving. "Where are you going now?" he asked me.

"I don't know. Why?" I said.

"I don't know," he said. "I guess I'm not really ready to go home."

"Me neither," I said. So we walked back over to Broadway, then started downtown. "Do you know where we're going?" he asked after we'd walked for a few blocks.

"No, unless you've got money," I said. "I only have a dollar left."

He checked his wallet. "Sixty-five cents and my bus pass," he said. "I guess we're just walking."

"*Brrrr!*" I shivered. I was wearing a skirt today and thin tights, and it had gotten very cold.

We were right outside Gregory's Coffee on Eighty-third Street. "Why don't we go in and ask for samples?" I said. "You can get free samples of the coffee of the day. Plus, if you answer the trivia question, they give you a free cup. Not the good stuff, like mochaccino or latte, but it's hot."

I happened to know that the highest lake in the world was Lake Titicaca, so we each got a sample-size hazelnut vanilla, and then we shared my free grande Sumatra. But after a few more minutes of walking, we were both shivering. "We could find another Gregory's," I suggested.

"Okay, there's one down around Seventy-fourth," he said. That one had no trivia contest, but the flavor of the day was Ethiopian and the kid gave us seconds.

It was getting dark really early these days. The wind off the river roared across Seventy-second Street. "It's really freezing. We should turn around," I said.

"Isn't there another Gregory's over by Lincoln Center?" he asked.

"Probably, but I have to be home at six," I said.

"Me, too," he said. "So we should turn around."

But we didn't, and when we reached the next Gregory's, I talked the guy into giving us one tall cup for free, instead of two of the tiny size. "Too bad they don't give out food samples in here," I said.

"Yeah," Max said, "we might need to start checking out grocery stores."

We'd been laughing all along, but as we pushed through the Lincoln Center crowds, passing the hot cup back and forth, our shoulders bumping as we took turns sipping from the opening in the cover, we got completely giddy. "You know," I said, "if we walk back on Columbus, we should hit at least one more Gregory's, maybe two."

"No, please!" he begged. "No more coffee!"

"Why? Just because you have a stomachache?" I was giggling.

He looked at me. "Seriously, do you, too?"

"It's not exactly feeling good," I said. "Have you started twitching yet?"

"Not twitching," he said, "but I'm feeling like I could fly home under caffeine power!"

I was flying, too, and it wasn't just caffeine.

He suddenly stopped walking. "Hey, isn't that your dog?" he said.

Surely there were many other grizzled, sausage-shaped terriers in green plaid dog coats on Broadway, but this one, tied to a parking meter in front of Fluffy's Cafe, was definitely Sarge.

He barked ecstatically when he saw us. "Don't look at him!" I said. "Keep walking."

"Too late," he said. "There's your uncle."

It was indeed Uncle Max, sitting in the window booth. "Uh-oh!" I said. He'd spotted us. He waved and knocked on the window, then, smiling broadly, beckoned us to come in. "You ready for this?" I asked Max.

"Probably not," he said.

Uncle Max was sitting with another man, empty plates and coffee cups in front of them. "Fancy meeting you here!" he said. "Hello there, Young Max. This is a big surprise. Sit down, sit down." They moved over to make room for us, but we stayed standing. I could hear Sarge yelping outside the door. I thought maybe if I didn't look at either Max, it might lessen the possibilities for embarrassment, so I began a search for an imaginary tissue. "Join the party. You want a cup of coffee?"

"What are you doing here?" I asked before he could ask us any questions.

"Sy and I were just chewing the fat," he said, "talking about the past, the present, the future, boasting about the grandchildren, or in my case, you." He smiled. "Joy, this is Sy Karetsky. Sy, my famous niece and her friend Max." He gave me a probing look and his eyebrow went up, but so quickly I don't know if they noticed.

"We weren't chewing the fat," said Sy Karetsky, who was approximately the same size, shape, and age as Uncle Max. "We were arguing."

"It wasn't an argument," said Uncle Max.

"Good, now we can argue about that." Sy Karetsky looked at me. "Joy, your uncle is without a doubt the stubbornest, most hardheaded—"

"Unlike certain other people I could name," said Uncle Max. "What it is, Sy keeps trying to rope me into starting up our old card game again, and I keep telling him what's the point when he's about to leave for Florida?"

"What rope?" said Sy. "Besides, Joy, I keep telling him—"

They were both clearly enjoying every minute of this. I, on the other hand, was desperate to get away before major embarrassment. I also didn't want to squander what little Max time I had left tonight with these two guys. I checked my watch, then looked at Max.

"You're right, Joy. What time is it?" said Uncle Max.

"Almost six," I said.

"We'd better go," he said. "Don't want to upset Ilene." He turned to Sy. "Ilene keeps me on a short leash, you know. Shorter than Joy's."

"That won't do," said Sy. "At least with a wife, over the years, with any luck, you get her trained."

"Nah," Uncle Max said as he stood up. "It suits me fine. She keeps me out of trouble."

"So do I get an A for effort?" he asked in the cab home, after we'd dropped Max at his door. He'd insisted that we all ride together. "I thought I was very well behaved, don't you? I didn't embarrass you. I didn't ask any nosy questions at all, right?"

"You were okay," I said.

He peered at me over the tops of his glasses. "So can I ask them now?"

I looked right back at him. "You don't like it when Mom wants to know your every move."

He gave me another appraising look. "And Sy thinks I'm feisty. . . . You're a regular chip off the old Mitnick block."

He dropped it, then. I just wondered for how long.

Chapter 25

"Are you going?" asked Max Monday morning as we passed the sign in the stairwell announcing the fall talent show.

"I don't know," I said.

"It's going to be pretty bad," he said. "It always is."

"I've never been to a school social event," I said.

"Oh, well, in that case," he said, "you should definitely go."

But I wasn't totally sure he was asking me till the next morning, when he said, "We could see who else wants to come along for this great evening of entertainment."

Jen said she could go, as did J.J. and John. Tara's parents asked her a million questions, but finally agreed. Mom and Dad said yes, too. I didn't mention Max to them. I just said a whole bunch of us were going. "Sounds fun," Mom said. "I'm glad you're going out. You, too, Max. It's good for you to get out and socialize." She'd been in a much better mood since she'd heard about his visit with Sy Karetsky.

"I'm doing it for Sarge," said Uncle Max. "He's the one who needs the change of pace. It's very depressing for him being cooped up in my room. Getting out is good for his spirits." I didn't know why he was still keeping Sarge locked up, since Nathan had stopped letting Kurt and Ludwig out of their cage, but I stayed clear of it. I was keeping a low profile, just trying to make it through till Friday.

By Friday, our group had grown to include Max's friend Mike as well. The show was at seven. We met at six thirty to make sure we could all sit together. "Okay," Max told me as we filed into the auditorium, "the basic principle behind this is, it's so bad it's good, so don't get your hopes up, okay?"

My hopes were already up, as were my mood and my pulse rate, but I nodded. I let everyone else go in first so I could sit next to him. Tara sat next to J.J. I'd noticed they'd seemed to be hitting it off really well lately. "Check it out!" I gave Jen, who was on the other side of me, a poke. "Looks like Tara's unlocking that inner babe after all."

She glanced at Max, then back at me. "She's not the only one!" I swatted her.

The auditorium was filling up now. We talked and laughed until the lights dimmed and a kid in jeans and an oversized blue suit jacket ambled out from behind the curtains. "Uh, hi," he said, "and welcome to the Fall Talent Show. We have a great evening of entertainment in store for you." He rolled his eyes. Max nudged me. "However, we do have a few last-minute program adjustments. The first act seems to have broken a string on his violin, so *Flight of the Bumblebee* will have to wait. Instead, we are proud to present"—he stopped to check his note card—"the amazing and talented, didn't drop anything at the rehearsal, and with any luck he won't tonight . . . Ladies and gentlemen, give it up for . . . Ju-u-u-stin-n-n the Jugg-ler!"

With that, the curtain parted, the audience clapped and whistled, and out stepped Justin Zuwadski. Wearing his Dr. Bunsen Honeydew shirt and huge black pants, biting his lip and frowning like his life was at stake, he juggled first three beanbags, then four, then five, then a bunch of bananas. Jen, Tara, and I cracked up. The harder he frowned, the more hysterical we got. "You know this guy?" Max asked.

"Since second grade," I said, gasping for breath. "His brother's Nathan's best friend."

"I don't know what you're laughing about," he said. "I wish I could juggle."

"We're laughing," Tara informed him, "because he has a huge crush on Joy."

"No, he's over it," I said. "Thank God."

"Too bad," Max said. "He could have taught you to juggle."

I punched him. He caught my hand and held it a little longer than he needed to. "And you said I was going to hate this," I told him.

After what must have been ten minutes of juggling, the next act came on—a girl singing and tap-dancing to "New York, New York." Next came a pathetic rap group, then a stand-up comic who was even worse, then two boys in red dresses and high heels who lip-synched to "Baby Love." We laughed through all but the tap dancer, who was trying so hard it would have been too mean. It wasn't till the emcee announced Polaris that I stopped laughing. In fact, my heart almost stopped.

It was Maple. Polaris was Wade's band. There was Wade, in a black knit hat pulled down over his ears, and Kim and the bass player and the drummer, who I didn't know, and Maple with a tambourine—all in their long rumpled coats. "They ought to call themselves Raincoat," Max said as they launched into a raunchy, punky, funky jumble of sound. Wade played lead guitar and sang. Maple shook the tambourine and joined in on the chorus. You couldn't understand a word they were singing—you could barely even hear them—but the audience loved it. On the next verse, she took off her coat, tossed it on the floor, and began to dance. "Look how tight that skirt is!" Jen yelled to me. "And that slit? Where do you even buy something like that?"

"In the mermaid supply catalog?" Tara shouted.

"You're right." Jen laughed. "She looks like a punk mermaid."

"Are they punk?" yelled Tara. "Is that what this is supposed to be?"

"Got me!" said Jen.

"She sure can't sing," Tara said, sticking her fingers in her ears.

"She's going to need to be surgically removed from that skirt," Jen yelled.

Their loyalty was great, but they were wrong. I loved the skirt—the way its turquoise sequins caught the light, and how she wore it with a stretchy black top, short, flat gold boots, and red tights, and how she'd dyed her hair—what little had grown in—a turquoise green to match. Plus the mere thought of being up there like that filled me with terror, and yet here she was, whooping and whirling, wiggling and prancing, shaking her tambourine like she'd been doing this her whole life.

"She's good!" Max said.

"She's great!" I said. I was too proud and astounded even to be jealous.

The audience clearly agreed. "More, more!" we all shouted when the song ended. The ones who weren't already on their feet got up and yelled and cheered. I got up along with them, as did Max and Mike and John and J.J. and eventually, even my wonderfully loyal friends Jen and Tara. And we stayed up, waving our arms and dancing along all through the next number. When that song ended, again we whistled and screamed for more. The band bowed and grinned, and waved and grinned. The drummer played a riff as Wade stepped forward. "Uh, we'd do another song," he said, "but we don't have one."

"But we'll be back!" Maple called. Maple the Rock Star, in her slinky mermaid skirt and funny gold booties and green fuzz. The jeers turned to cheers.

"Did you know she could do that?" Max asked as the curtains closed and the emcee announced intermission. All around us, kids headed up the aisles, moving toward the doors.

"Are you kidding!" I said. "She was amazing!"

"Uh-oh, here they come!" Tara leaned across Jen to tell me as Maple and Wade came through the stage door into the auditorium. Kids rushed over, crowding around them, slapping Wade on the back, hugging Maple, but the two of them kept walking right toward us, Wade in front, Maple behind him, holding his hand, still with that I'm-great smile but edgy now as they got closer to us.

"Are you going to say anything to her?" asked Jen.

My heart fluttered.

Wade stopped right in front of Max, who was on the aisle. "Whew!" he said, pulling off his hat and fanning his face with it. "So what'd you think?"

"Great!" Max said. "You guys were fantastic!"

"Maple was fantastic." Wade put his arm around her and pulled her next to him. She made a face, but then smiled up at him.

"You really were," Max said.

"Thanks." She smiled at him, then gave a quick glance at me. I saw her tighten as she waited to see if I would say something.

"You were so good!" I told her.

This time her eyes stayed on me. "I didn't look too stupid up there?"

"What are you, kidding?" I said. "They loved you. You could have done a whole set, they loved it so much. I didn't know you could do that!"

"Neither did I," she said. "But I figure, I can't play, I can't sing real well, I might as well jump around."

It was happening. The ice had broken. But now what?

Wade looked at me and Max, then at Maple, then at me again. "Listen," he said. "We're going to split now. Do you two maybe want to come along?"

Max gave me a questioning look. I looked at Maple, who shot a glance at me, then looked away. "Yeah," I said. "Okay."

"Great," Wade said. "I'm ravenous. Let's get pizza."

It was a five-block walk to Sal's. I couldn't believe two people so completely draped around each other could walk so fast. "Yo, Wade!" Max called. "I thought you gave up track. Think you can slow it down?"

"I didn't know you guys even knew each other," I said.

"Yeah," Max said, "we were on the track team together in junior high."

"I hope this doesn't get too weird," I said. It was as hard staying even with them as it was keeping up with all this stuff going on. "Should I bring up the fight, or ask how she's been all these weeks, or do I just try acting normal, whatever that means?"

"Just be yourself," he said.

"That's how the whole thing happened in the first place, remember?" I said. "If we get into another big fight, will you break it up?"

"Look at her," Max told me. "Does that look like somebody who's looking for a fight? Or even thinking about you?"

He was right. Even after we'd sat down and ordered, they were so busy rehashing the performance, planning their next one, and worrying about how soon till they could have more songs, it was almost as if we weren't there. When our pizza came, Wade and Max tore into it, but Maple blotted her slice with her napkin, then asked Wade for his napkin and swabbed that one in the grease, too. Then she picked off tiny bits of cheese and nibbled at them. I watched Max watching her.

"Maple, that's disgusting," I said.

"She always does that," Wade said.

No, she doesn't, I almost said. She never does that! But I'd have looked pretty stupid arguing with Wade over which one of us was better acquainted with Maple's eating habits. Besides, Max had caught my eye, so I let it go. "I like your hair," I told her.

She stopped pulling at her pizza and looked up at me. "You predicted it, Joy, remember? You predicted my hair would be green when we were filling out that Match Quiz. Remember that?" I nodded. It felt like a hundred years ago. "Wade's thinking of making his green, too, but less turquoise, more like lime or something. Right, Wade?" She kissed him for about the twentieth time since we'd been there. "And we're thinking of changing our names to Mint and Sage."

"Which one'll be which?" Max asked.

"We haven't decided." She looked at Max. "Listen, does anyone here care if I take off my boots? They've been killing me all night."

We all said it was fine. "They're cool boots," Max added.

"Yeah, they're great," I said.

"I know," she nodded. "I love these boots, but they

don't fit. Ooh, hey!" She looked up from unlacing them. "That sounds like the beginning of a song. Whaddaya think?" She dropped her voice an octave and went into a sort of pseudo-rap: "I love these boots but they don't fit—"

Wade jumped in: "They make my feet feel like—"

"Uh-uh!" Max gave them the thumbs down. "Bad, guys. Really bad."

"It's not that bad!" Maple protested. "It just needs work."

"Okay. How's this, then?" Max lowered his voice, too. "I love my boots, but they don't love me. It's too bad they weren't free. But I need to wear them 'cause I need to be cool. . . ." He paused and looked at me.

So I threw in: "Even if my toes think I'm a fool."

We were laughing, but Wade flopped back, groaning. "And you thought ours was bad! Don't quit your day job."

"Okay." Maple held up her hands. "We have another idea, right, Wade? This one's for real, though. It's not stupid. We started working on it last night. It's called Float."

"As in root beer?" I said. "I could get into that."

"No!" she said. "I told you, this one's serious. We're trying to do this whole sort of balloon-cloud metaphor—floating, drifting, bursting, that sort of thing—but we sort of got stuck after the first line—"

"Well, yeah," I said. "What rhymes with float besides bloat and goat?"

"There's devote," she said, gazing at Wade. "But we decided it doesn't have to rhyme."

"That's probably wise," said Max. "I mean, boat, moat, groat—it's not that promising, or all that sad."

"There's always 'you float my boat,'" I suggested. "Or has that been done?"

"Fine, mock me!" she said. "Maybe you and Max should write our songs with us. Or for us." She laughed. We were all laughing now. We laughed the whole way through the pizza—about the talent show, about Justin the Juggler, about the other customers. It just seemed as if everything cracked us up. Before I knew it, it was time for me to go.

"I should leave, too," Max said. We both stood up.

"You know, we should do this again," Wade said.

"Yeah." Maple looked at me. "Yeah, it was fun."

"It was," I agreed.

"So call me," she said.

"Amazing!" I told Max as soon as we were out the door. "It's a miracle. It went well, don't you think? It was actually fun!" Dad had given me money for a cab, but there was no way I could go home yet. Max didn't look ready to go home either, so we started walking. "I thought for sure we'd have to have this whole huge, heavy talk, but it seems like our fight's over. I forgot how much I liked Maple!"

He nodded. "Maple's okay."

"I like Wade a lot, too," I said. "And the pizza was excellent." Everything in life felt excellent to me at the moment.

"Yeah, Wade's a good guy," he said. "Put them together, though . . ." He rolled his eyes. "I mean, I can see what got you so pissed. They're out of their minds. It's beyond derangement. They're gaga. They're totally around the bend. Forget the songs. Did you notice how neither one of them wanted to know a single thing about you or me?"

It was all true. But I felt a lightness I hadn't felt since the fight. I wanted to grab Max's hand and skip the whole way home. Is that because I'm gaga, too? I wondered. But no, that wasn't it. Or if it was, it wasn't because of him. In case he'd picked up on it, though, I tried to make my face look serious. "This is so strange," I said. "I mean, she's no different than she was before, maybe even a little worse 'cause of the whole rock-star thing, but I don't know why, for some reason, it just didn't bother me. Aside from that revolting way she eats, nothing bothered me. D'you know what I mean?"

"Yeah, I do." Max nodded. "It's because you don't need her the same way you did."

"I mean, I still like her," I said. "She's fun. I still want to be friends. It's just—"

"Onward and upward, right?" he said.

That was it. Exactly.

Chapter 26

Maple had said I should call her. But we'd barely finished breakfast the next morning when she called. "Hey, I like Max," she said, as if we'd been talking every day. No "hi, hello, how're you doing." No "This is Maple." "That was fun last night," she said. "Max is great."

I brought the phone into the computer closet, even though Mom and Dad were just going out the door with Nathan to buy a parka. "Yeah, it was," I said.

"Wade likes you, too," she said. "He thinks you're funny and nice. So, since Thursday's Thanksgiving, I was wondering if the two of you want to double with us Wednesday night."

I'd barely calmed down from last night. Max and I had walked way longer than we should have, talking about friendship, gossiping, laughing, making up songs even worse than the boot rap. Now I felt another huge surge of excitement. I had to tell her, though. "You know," I said, "it's not like we're dating. Max and I aren't going out. We're just good friends."

"That's too bad," she said. "You should do something about that. He's seriously cute."

That was pure Maple—totally certain, and completely, totally oblivious. But it was so friendly, too. That was the thing about her. "I'll have to see if Max wants to go," I said.

"He'll want to go," she said. "This is too good to miss. We're going to go watch them blow up the balloons for the parade. It's over by the museum. It's, like, a whole scene. I never did that, did you?"

I'd seen the parade on TV every year and been to it a few times, but I'd never watched the balloons being blown up. It sounded absolutely great. But could Max stand another evening with them? Did I even dare to ask? Plus the date aspect sort of worried me. I'd have to figure out how to present this to him. Maple obviously was the wrong person to discuss it with. I needed to consult with Jen and Tara. But just then Uncle Max knocked on the door. "Joy! You said you'd be right back," he called. "What's the holdup? I can't get him in the tub all by myself."

"Just a minute," I called back. There was no point ignoring him. He'd just get louder. "Maple," I said, "I gotta go. I promised I'd help Uncle Max give Sarge a bath."

"Okay," she said. "Call Max and call me back!"

Uncle Max had Sarge on his leash when I came out. He looked very out of sorts. I tried explaining how I'd seen Maple last night and that the fight was over, but he had no interest. The only thing on his mind was pulling Sarge toward the bathroom. The only thing on Sarge's mind was not to budge. "I tried to trick him into thinking we were going for a walk," he said as Sarge, who had all four legs braced, resisted with all his strength. "I got the leash on him, but he must have heard me run the water. Plus I'm sure he noticed I don't have on my coat and hat. Look at him!" Sarge was leaning backward so hard now he was almost sitting down. "He looks like he's about to face the firing squad. You'd better pick him up."

"Fine." I hoped it didn't take too long to wash a dog. I needed to reach Jen and Tara before they both went out. Sarge did not like being picked up, and for a small dog, he weighed a ton, but he let me tote him to the bathroom. "What now?" I said, eyeing the sudsy water in the bottom of the tub.

"Put him in! Goo-o-o-d Sarge! It's not as bad as you think," he said as I deposited Sarge in the water. Sarge gave me a last No-Mama-you-can't-mean-it! look, then scrabbled frantically as his nails slipped on the wet porcelain. But then it seemed as if he relaxed, so I straightened up. "Oy! What are you doing?" cried Uncle Max.

"You can't let go of him! He'll jump out! Stay, Sarge! Good boy! Come on, Joy, hold him tighter!"

"I'm trying!" I kneeled down on the tiles. "Sarge! Sit! Stay! Lie down!"

Not on your life! Sarge's eyes said back. So I hooked my elbow around his neck and held on as Uncle Max got the plastic cup, towels, washcloth, and dog shampoo and sat down on Nathan's baby stool. "It'd be easier to keep hold of him if you'd left the stupid lampshade on," I said. I was already dripping wet.

"Yes, well, I'm hoping the bath will help his skin. That's a good boy. See, nobody's gonna murder you." Sarge flinched as Uncle Max dumped water over him. "Come on, Joy, keep his head up for me and we'll be in business."

Now that I had him in the headlock, it was going fine. Uncle Max and I were soaked, but Sarge was getting washed. He looked pathetic. The wet hair around his ears stuck out like chicken feathers, while the long ones on his chin and belly hung down in limp strings. Uncle Max gave him a pat, then shook his head. "And you were so cute as a pup," he said.

"And why exactly are we doing this?" I asked, trying to arrange my legs in a more comfortable position.

"Certain parties have been complaining that he smells," he said. "Me, I don't smell it, but I bow to their sharper noses."

"Why now, though?"

"We're going visiting later. I want to make sure he has plenty of time to dry."

"Where you going?" I asked.

"Where else?" He raised an eyebrow. "Rose's."

"So I guess you'll finally get to eat all that Chinese stuff she froze," I said.

"Oh," he said, squirting more shampoo onto the washcloth, "we ate that long ago."

Hmmm. Had I missed something here? I stopped thinking about what to say to Max. "When?"

"I don't know." He shrugged. "A while back. We had it for lunch one day."

"One day?" Implying he ate lunch with her more than one day? "You didn't tell me that."

"What? I have to tell you everything?"

Fine, I'd back off. "Was it good?"

"It was all right."

On the other hand, this was too interesting to totally back off. "So, then, you"—I debated how to put it—"eat lunch with Rose?"

"Occasionally," he said.

That would be just our luck, if something were starting to happen with Rose now, when she was leaving. "What's this tonight?" I asked. "Do Mom and Dad know?"

"Oy! Listen to this, Sarge! Miss Nosy Parker!"

"I'm not nosy," I said, "I'm just interested."

He chuckled. Or snorted. "That line's worthy of me," he said. "I hate to tell you, it's hardly a hot date. It's a whole dinner party, a pre-Florida good-bye or some such, people I don't even know, plus the Karetskys and Mrs. Posner, who I'm not that fond of. I told her, I don't know why you're in such a big hurry to spend time with Mimi Posner. You're going to be stuck next door to her all winter. I think that may have annoyed her a little bit, which is another reason I decided to spiff up the pooch."

"The pooch looks like he's sunk into a deep depression," I said. I'd long since released Sarge from the headlock, and he hadn't moved. "We shouldn't have done this to him. He hates it. You could have left him home."

"Nah." Uncle Max scratched him between the ears. "He'll get over it. Sarge is a party animal. By tonight, he'll have forgotten all about it. Besides, now maybe Marty'll stop making all those smelly dog cracks. And yes, I told them that I'm going out. Believe me, they're only too glad to be rid of me for an evening! If they have an ounce of sense, they'll go out themselves." He looked at me. "You're not upset Rose didn't invite you this time, are you? We didn't think you'd want to come to an old folks' get-together. My guess is all I'm going to hear about is Florida. They're leaving in a week.

Besides"—he got that gleam in his eye, the gleam I knew and feared—"I figured you'd be going out with a certain young man whose name begins with M and ends with—"

I looked up at him. "I'm not, quote, going out with Max."

"Well, you looked pretty cute together the other day."

This was two times I'd heard the word cute, and two times I'd had to make this same announcement in one morning.

"Don't get excited!" he said. "How long is it now that I didn't bring it up? Never mind in front of anybody. I've turned over a new leaf, in case you didn't notice. You want to have a secret life, that's your business."

"Max and I are friends," I said. "Just because I don't tell everyone every single thing, it doesn't mean I have a secret life. Speaking of secret life, by the way, I don't see you telling anybody—"

"Telling anybody what?" This was a definite snort. "That I'm eating Yankee bean soup with Sy Karetsky?"

I looked at him. "That's what you do every day?"

"Not always. Sometimes I have the turkey special, but it's usually too dry."

There was a blob of shampoo on my arm. I flicked it at him. It landed on his glasses.

"Hey, watch it!" he said.

Sarge snapped to attention, as if he wasn't sure if we were fooling around or getting into something. I wasn't sure either. Uncle Max took off his glasses and dried them on the towel. He put them back on, folded his arms, and looked down at me. "Fine, you want to know what I do every day?" he said. The needling, teasing tone was gone now. "I go and sit in my apartment. I throw out whatever Chinese restaurant menus they've shoved under the door, I pull the dead leaves off the begonias, I look through my old papers, once a week I run the carpet sweeper, once in a while I drop in and see Rose. Sometimes I eat lunch in the coffee shop. This way I'm not in everyone's hair here all day long, I'm not getting on anybody's nerves, and I still feel like I have a semblance of a life."

"You have a life," I said. "You have a life here." I knew I sounded just like Mom, but I had to say something. He gave a resigned sort of shrug, which made me even sadder. It also made me want to tell him something in return. So I told him about Maple and the talent show. "We seem to have made up," I said.

That perked him up a little. "That's good news."

"Yeah." I nodded. "I think. She's just as wrapped up in Wade, though. They're both gaga. Plus now she wants to be a rock star."

He shrugged again. "What're you going to do?

Except for us old fossils, everybody changes. Sometimes for the better, sometimes not. And as long as you're still friends, onward and upward."

"That's just what Max said," I said.

"Max is a smart boy."

"So . . . Maple wants me to go with them to watch the Thanksgiving Day Parade balloons blown up," I said.

"Oh, yeah? I used to do that years back," he said. "Over by the Museum of Natural History, right?" I nodded. "Yeah, I went with my brother and his family. Do they still have the Mickey Mouse balloon? And Woody Woodpecker? I don't know why, I was always partial to Woody Woodpecker—"

"She wants me to ask Max," I said.

"That sounds like fun," he said. "You going to?"

"I feel a little funny about it," I said.

"Why? These days the girl can ask the boy, right?"

"Yes, but I don't know if I should call him or wait till school, or what. He might say no."

Uncle Max looked like that was the stupidest thing he'd ever heard. "He's not going to say no. He's not crazy. A girl like you . . ."

"He might get the wrong idea."

"You ask me, it's the right idea."

"It's not like that," I said for the too-manyeth time. "I told you, we're just good friends."

"Nothing wrong with friends," he said. "Friends is good. Good friends is even better. People should have more good friends. That's what Rose and I are, for your information."

"What?" He'd taken me by surprise.

"That's what you've been itching to find out, isn't it?"

I had no idea what to say.

"Come on," he said, "you think I didn't notice all your facilitating? You know"—he gave me a wry smile—"facilitating—like what I did with Leland? And with Max, for that matter."

I felt my face redden. "I didn't know you knew."

He put a hand on my shoulder. "Joy, darling, subtlety is not your strong point. Sweet, yes. Subtle, no. Unlike, for example, me."

"Well, anyway," I said, "it didn't work."

"What do you want? You gave yourself a tough assignment. It's one thing to try to be a matchmaker, another to be a magician." He shook his head and sighed. "Oy, Joy! Look what it's come to—the two of us sitting here, covered with dog shampoo, discussing our love life. . . ."

"You mean lack of love life," I said.

"That actually depends on your definition. There's no lack of love. And we're still alive, last time I checked." He leaned over and gave me a rough kiss on the head. "Anyway, a word to the wise, in case it should come up. I may have told you this before. With relationships, it's very important: Get in very slowly . . ."

"I know, I know," I said, "and get out very fast. Hey!" I looked up from what had turned into this sort of awkward hug. "Not you, Sarge!"

It was too late. Sarge had scrambled out of the tub and was shaking himself all over. Water flew off him like it was fired from a Super Soaker. I grabbed him and wrapped him in the one dry towel. He shimmied around until he got it unwrapped, whereupon he shook off the rest of the water. Far from being annoyed, Uncle Max looked proud. "Look at him!" he said, pointing and laughing. "Look what he just did! This dog isn't over the hill at all. He facilitated himself right out of there. And now you're ready to boogie, right, boy?" Sarge wagged his stringy stub of a tail. "Joy, help me get up from this stool. Then go call Max. Then, if you're not doing anything, maybe you'll bake me a nice cake to bring to Rose."

Chapter 27

I managed to throw together your basic cake while I was on the phone—with Tara, then Jen, then Maple again—but by the time I'd worked out what to say to Max, I'd eaten three quarters of the batter. "The whole thing's sort of a research project, is the way I understand it," I told him as I got out the ingredients for another batch, which we had, luckily. "You know, research for the Float song?"

"I see," he said. "Well, I'm into research."

This was much easier than I'd imagined. "Great!" I said.

But my elation didn't last. At first I thought it was batter poisoning, or possibly the pizza, but by Saturday night, I had a nasty cold. "Don't worry," Uncle Max said. "I'll call Rose and tell her I can't come." Mom and Dad had taken his advice and gone out for an early movie and then dinner. "I'll stay here and make a soup for you and Nathan. Rose will understand."

"After we spent all that time washing Sarge? No way," I said. "You're going."

So he took Sarge and the cake, and I spent the evening lying on the couch, blowing my nose and praying whatever this was would be gone by Monday. Mom and Dad were home by nine. Uncle Max didn't get back till almost ten thirty. "I tried to get away earlier," he said, "but they wouldn't let me."

"You must have been having a pretty good time, then," Mom said. She and Dad had spent all afternoon saying how wonderful Sarge looked and smelled and how terrific it was that Uncle Max was going out.

"I hope they appreciated the new, improved Sarge," I said.

"Oh, Sarge was a big hit," he said, hanging his cane on the doorknob, then taking off his hat and coat, "and Rose made a good dinner, and they loved the cake per usual, but Sy is very hard to talk to. God almighty, that man is pushy." Mom and Dad exchanged looks. I had to agree with them. He'd never change. At least he'd stopped making derogatory comments about Rose. "It was exactly as I predicted, Joy," he said. "Florida this, Florida that, on and on. To hear them talk, you'd think New York City was the Black Hole of Calcutta. At least Mrs. Posner wasn't there. She's having health problems of some sort. How're you feeling, by the way? You look terrible."

"I feel terrible," I said.

"You can't be sick for Wednesday. Not when things are going so excellently."

Sunday, Mom made Nathan clear out so I could spend the day in bed. I was no better Monday. At least once an hour, Uncle Max came in to offer tea with honey or orange juice or chicken soup or vitamin C, and ask if my throat still hurt, and if I had a fever. "Oh, are you sleeping?" he said each time. "Sorry. I heard you blowing your nose, so I assumed you were awake. Don't blow so hard! It isn't good for you." It got annoying fast. "What're you barking at me for?" he protested. "I'm just trying to get you better for your date."

"I'll be better," I said. "And stop calling it a date. It doesn't help."

I hadn't really expected to hear from Max over the weekend, but I was sure he'd call after school Monday. He didn't, though, or Tuesday either. I jumped each time the phone rang, but it was always either one of my other friends, calling with the homework or words of wisdom, or it was for Uncle Max. "You're a popular fellow, Max," Dad said. "I had no idea."

"Yes, well," he said, "you know how Joy has her people. I seem to have my people, too. And at the moment they all seem to have a lot to say."

By Tuesday night I was really worried. Maple had

told him Monday that I was sick. She said she'd also told him that I was definitely still going Wednesday night, and that he'd said he was still planning to come. So then why hadn't he called? The worst part of being sick is that you have nothing to do but lie there and make up theories. My friends thought I was stupid not calling him, but by now it felt too weird.

Wednesday morning, when I woke up still feeling crummy, I was in despair. I dressed for school, though, and came in to breakfast. There was only half a day today. I had to find out what was going on. "If you don't feel good, don't go in," Uncle Max said when I told him and Mom what I was thinking. "Don't despair. This can still work out."

"How?" I looked at Mom. "If I don't go to school, you know Mom's not going to let me go out."

"If you rest up all day and you feel all right, she'll let you go. Right, Ilene? You'll let her go. She'll have four days to rest up afterward."

"I don't know," said Mom, who had a box of tissues beside her coffee cup and looked to be in a pretty bad mood herself. "I'm going to be very upset if this whole family's sick for Thanksgiving, which, by the way, I haven't done a thing about yet."

"What does that have to do with the price of cheese?" he said. "Besides, where is it written, Ilene, that you have to knock yourself out making a turkey dinner? It's not as if there are other people coming. It's just the five of us this year, right? I don't even like turkey."

"That's not the point," she said. "We have such a small family, and so few traditions."

"Fine," he said, "then we can order the turkey. If you're still under the weather, we'll order everything. You won't have to lift a finger. I'll treat. Joy can tell you, I'm a facilitator. Right, Joy?" He gave me a big wink.

"I hate to tell you," I said. "I need more than a turkey facilitator. I need a miracle."

"Who's talking about turkey?" he said.

And, in fact, I got my miracle. We were just clearing up from breakfast when the phone rang. "I thought for sure you'd be on the bus today," Max said. He sounded worried. "You must be really sick."

My heart swelled. "I'm not that bad," I said. "Where are you?"

"Just about to go in to school," he said. "So does this mean we're not doing this tonight?"

"No." I looked at Mom, and then at Uncle Max. "I may be better by then. I'll call you later."

Miracle two was that I was. Uncle Max credited it to his chicken soup, four vitamin C pills, a grapefruit, three glasses of orange juice, and four cups of tea with lemon and honey. I thought it was sheer force of will.

Miracle three was that Dad overruled Mom, and said that if I bundled up and came home early, I could go. So I put on two thick pairs of socks, my warm boots, my winter jacket, a knit hat, and a big wool scarf, and brought along two packs of tissues, and at seven o'clock, we met on Max's corner.

I couldn't believe how happy I was to be outside again. Or how glad I was to see him. I thought he looked pretty glad to see me, too. Maple and Wade, who had on those large, funny multicolored jester hats as well as their trusty raincoats, were in a great mood also, and by the time we joined the people streaming toward the museum, I felt like we were going to a carnival. The crowds completely filled the sidewalks and the steps of the museum—kids, grown-ups, parents with strollers, guys carrying little kids in snowsuits on their shoulders, tourists speaking all different languages. They pressed up against the barricades, spilled over into the park, everyone all squashed together, bumping into everybody else. But it wasn't like on the subway. Everyone was having a great time. Boom boxes blared. Kids yelled. Walkie-talkies crackled. It was like a gigantic party. A very cold, extremely windy party. "This is great!" I shouted.

"Yeah, look at those tank trucks!" Maple shouted back. She pointed down Seventy-seventh Street, where dozens, maybe hundreds of guys in hooded sweatshirts and red coveralls with MACY'S on the back scurried around attaching things, securing things, arranging things. "Look how big those hoses are! Oh, cool, they're pumping up the Pink Panther! See how he's puffing up? How much helium do you think one of those things takes?"

"A lot!" Wade said. "That dude is huge! And look, there's Snoopy!"

There were all the balloons I'd seen in every Thanksgiving Day Parade since I was a little girl—Big Bird, Sonic the Hedgehog, Kermit, Mickey—some already blown up, straining against their ropes, bobbing and bouncing in the wind, others laid out in the street, ready to go. "Look!" I nudged Max and pointed to an enormous purple thing. "They're unfolding Barney! This is so cool." Max nodded. We worked our way close enough to see a bunch of workers spreading out the Barney balloon in the middle of the street, then smoothing it and covering it with netting. A rowdy guy next to me was wearing one of those very large fur hats with earflaps and a sweatshirt that said WOSSAMOTTA U. Next to him an old couple passed a thermos back and forth. "This is so great," I said again. "I feel like I'm six."

"Me, too!" Maple shouted back.

"Barney will do that to you," Max said. I hadn't noticed till then that he was the only one who didn't seem completely into this. He was sort of standing there, his hands jammed in his pockets.

"Are you cold?" I said. I was feeling completely fine.

"No, I'm okay," he said.

"Look, down there toward the park!" Wade pointed. "They're working on Garfield!" Sure enough, a guy on a huge ladder was climbing Garfield's face. "C'mon, let's go over there."

"What?" Max said.

"Garfield. The cat. Over there!" Maple shouted. "Max, hello? Are you still with us? Join the world."

"Huh? Oh, yeah, I'm all right," Max said.

"Do you hate this?" Maple asked him.

"No, I like it," he said.

"Well, then, let's go look at Garfield." She linked her arm through mine. "C'mon, Joy, let's go."

Max looked at me. "How 'bout if we meet you over there?" he told her.

"That's cool." She gave me a not-at-all-subtle look. "Have fun!"

"We'll never find them again," I said as they were swallowed up in the crowd.

"That's okay," he said.

"They're really getting to you, huh?" I said. "They're not bothering me at all tonight. But that could be because I've just been let out of my cage."

"No, they're okay," he said. "I've just sort of got something on my mind." He suddenly seemed fidgety and edgy, as if he wished he could be anywhere but here.

"Is something wrong?" I said.

"Not really." He'd stopped looking at me. "I guess I'm just feeling a little weird."

"So should we leave?" I asked. " 'Cause I don't think they'll care." He shook his head. "Max?" I was nervous now. "What's going on? You going to tell me?"

"I can't say it with ten thousand people listening," he said.

We threaded our way to the edge of the crowd. "What is it?" I said.

He looked down at his shoes. "I'm scared," he said.

"About?"

I saw him swallow. "You," he said. "I know I should have called while you were sick. That's why I didn't call."

My stomach dropped. He knew. And now he was going to dump me. I stopped breathing.

"You want to go get a hot dog or something?" he asked.

"No," I said. I'd been too pushy, that was it. I'd changed the rules. This was too much like a date, especially with the Raincoat Twins. It was pressure. And now he thought I'd gone gaga on him. "You might as well just say it."

"Yeah, I know," he said. "I'm sorry. I'm going to be really upset if I screw this up. We're friends, right, you and me?"

"Of course we're friends," I said.

"I know." He nodded. "And we're doing so well this way. Like, normal abnormal. We know how to do it. We've got it down, which is fairly amazing, don't you think?" I nodded, too. A dull ache was starting in my chest. "I mean, I never had a real friend who was a girl before—"

"I knew it," I said, before he could say more. "I shouldn't have done this. It's my fault. It was a bad idea. That's why I didn't call you either. But you don't have to worry, okay? You said it to me in the beginning—no basket cases, no more romantic swamps. I totally agree. I'm not about to screw this up!"

"Who said anything about you?" He was almost shouting suddenly. "It's not you I'm worried about. You can handle this. You're well balanced— No, you are," he said. "You have friends, you have a life, you have your art." Was I hearing him correctly? Had I lost my mind? "I know, I put that really pompously, but it's true, Joy, you're so solid and down-to-earth. . . ."

"Me?" My voice sounded as if I'd been hooked to

one of those helium trucks. I felt about as solid and down-to-earth as Sonic the Hedgehog over there bobbling in the wind.

"You are," he said again. "That's what I love about you."

The word seemed to slip out of his mouth so easily, but once out, it hung there. I didn't dare look at him. Neither one of us said anything—in my case, because my lips had gone numb and my ears boomed like there were two giant seashells clamped over them.

Max took a deep breath and blew it out. "So it looks like I did screw everything up," he said. "I'm sorry."

"I'm not sorry," I said. He still had his hands jammed in his jacket pockets. I put my hand in with his. A minute ago that would have seemed like the most forward thing I'd done in my whole life. Now it felt exactly right.

But now what? We stood there like that for a while, neither one of us knowing what to say. Finally he said, "So what do you think? You think we can do this without being totally deranged?"

I don't know what I answered. But I could have said anything and he would not have heard. "Yo! Yo! Look over there!" It sounded like that same guy from WOSSA-MOTTA U again, shouting.

"Oh, wow!" the kids alongside of me were yelling.

"Mommy, *mira!*" screamed a little kid.

"It's Bullwinkle! They're blowing up Bullwinkle!"

"Yo, Bullwinkle!"

"Bull-winkle! Bull-winkle! Bull-winkle!"

A giant roar rose from the crowd. But I wasn't watching. They could have been launching a moon rocket instead of inflating a moose, and I still would have missed all of it. Because Max was kissing me.

Chapter 28

So this is what derangement felt like.

I thought I handled it extremely well, though. I said, "Wow!" a lot more times than I'd have wished, but otherwise, I don't think I was much less cool than usual. I didn't melt into a puddle on Seventy-seventh and Columbus, or blush or simper when we found Wade and Maple over by Peter Rabbit, though they were so far into their own derangement I'm not sure they would have noticed. I didn't bump into any streetlights, walking home, or step into any open manholes, even after we stopped to kiss along the way. I managed to give Mom and Dad and Uncle Max, who unfortunately were all in the living room watching the eleven o'clock news, a reasonable description of the evening without them asking why I had that moony smile on my face. And when I dug the Kestrel notebooks out from under my bed at two twenty-five (I couldn't sleep, but Nathan, mercifully, had slept over at the Zuwadskis', so I had the room to myself), I didn't write *MAX MAX MAX Joy loves Max* all over it. I drew until my eyes shut.

I woke up almost as soon as it got light but lay in bed till really late. I wouldn't see him till Monday. He'd given me his grandmother's number in Connecticut, though, and I knew he'd call. It was a good bet Maple would soon call, too, but I didn't want to talk to anyone. This feeling wasn't for sharing. It was for savoring quietly, alone. I hugged my pillow, replaying the entire evening, remembering every touch, every word. Max thought I was solid and down-to-earth, so maybe this wasn't derangement I was feeling now. Maybe it was happiness.

Way before I was ready to join the world, Uncle Max knocked on the door. "Rise and shine, Joy!" he called. "It's after eleven." He opened the door and stuck his head in. "So, anything new and exciting to report? You looked pretty pleased with yourself last night. Do I have to mind my own business, or can I ask?" My face must have given it away, because he smiled. "That good, huh? How's the cold? It better not be worse or I'll catch hell."

My nose seemed manageable. My throat didn't hurt. "I'm good," I said.

"Excellent!" he said. "Because I've given Ilene and Marty the day off. I sent them out for breakfast and told them not to come back till the afternoon. Nathan won't be back till after the parade. I've ordered quite a dinner for us. We'd better get to work."

I'm sure it was a delicious dinner. Uncle Max certainly ordered enough food. But all I can remember is the conversation. Nathan started it. "Every time I'm at the Zuwadskis' and Justin's there?" he said. "All he talks about is Joy. You're, like, his goddess. It's getting sickening. You should just go out with him, Joy, and let him get to know you so he can get over it."

"Yes, well, eat your heart out, Justin!" Uncle Max said before I could say anything. "The girl's spoken for. You can tell Justin he'd better get in line. Right, Joy?"

"Oh, yeah?" Nathan put down his turkey leg. "You're still in love with Max?"

All eyes focused on me. I focused on my mashed potatoes.

"How'd you know that? I thought only I knew," Uncle Max said to Nathan. "I thought it was a deep, dark secret."

"It's the first I'm hearing," Dad said.

"I know everything," said Nathan. "He was over here that day."

"What day? What'd I miss?" asked Uncle Max.

"You mean way back when school started?" asked Mom. "This is the same Max from your match list, Joy? That dark, shy, good-looking—"

"I certainly remember him!" Dad nodded, grinning. "Sarge's friend."

"He seemed very nice." Mom was smiling, too.

I'd been trying to keep from smiling. Now I gave it up. "He is," I said.

"He's a class act," said Uncle Max. "And you know who picked him off the match list, right? Out of all twenty names?"

"No gloating," I said.

"Oh, come on," Dad said. "You have to let him gloat a little. I think his matchmaking was first-rate." He poked me. "You sure kept quiet about it, though."

"Uh-huh!" Nathan nodded. "And that's not the only time he was over here." He clearly liked being in the know even more than Uncle Max did. "He was here that day Sarge tried to eat Kurt and Ludwig."

Not that again.

"How'd that happen anyway?" Dad said. "I never really heard."

I figured with everything else coming out, I might as well admit it. "I sicced Sarge on them," I said. "I was just fooling around. I never really thought he'd do it."

"What do you mean, sicced him?" Uncle Max said. "You can't sic Sarge on anything. What, you think he's a hunter, or a guard dog?"

"He attacked, though," I said.

"Maybe, but he doesn't know from sic 'em," Uncle

Max said. "Where would he have learned sic 'em? Not from me, unless I have a secret life as a night watchman or a raccoon hunter." The thought made me giggle. "Watch this. I'll show you. Sarge!" He spoke sharply. Sarge looked up. "Sarge, sic 'em!"

Sarge looked at him blankly.

"See what I mean?" he said. "Nothing." He held out his hand. "You're a good boy, Sarge. Go back to sleep." But when Sarge toddled over, he handed him a Brussels sprout.

"You're feeding him at the table?" Mom said as Sarge gobbled it.

"It's a holiday," he said. "It's a special occasion."

Mom shook her head. "Max," she said, "you and Sarge certainly have kept things lively around here."

"Well . . ." he said. This whole time we'd been talking about Max and Sarge, he'd been looking more and more mischievous. Now he got this sort of coy, almost embarrassed look on his face. "You're about to have a small break from all the liveliness. Can anyone suggest a good place to buy a bathing suit?"

We all stopped eating.

"What?"

"What are you talking about?"

"Where are you going?"

"You're going to Florida? With Rose?" That was me, of course.

"Are you joking?"

"Since when? When did this come about?"

Uncle Max held up both hands like a traffic cop. "Don't get so excited. It's only for ten days. Sy talked me into it. He's a bossy guy, Sy. Worse than me. They've all been after me for a while, talking about getting a regular card game going down there, but ever since Saturday, when we found out Mimi Posner won't be going down for a few weeks because she's going in for an operation, and he came up with this idea of me borrowing her condo, he's been unbearable."

My head was still spinning from Max and me being a couple. Now Uncle Max going to Florida? "This is fantastic," I said. "It's so wonderful!"

"We'll see how wonderful it is," he said. "It's free."

"Do they allow dogs?" Dad asked.

"Well, Mimi takes her yappy little poodle," he said. "So yes. We'll have to see what Sarge has to say about all this. He's never flown."

"When did all this happen?" Mom asked again. "You could have said something."

"There was nothing to say," he said. "I didn't decide definitely till yesterday."

So that's why the phone had been ringing constantly.

Dad shook his head. "Oh, Max! You sly dog!"

"You're really going to Florida with Rose?" I said.

Uncle Max gave us an in-your-dreams-sweetheart!

look. "Let's get this straight," he said. "Next door is not the same as with."

"Mrs. Posner's apartment is right next door to Rose's?" I'd forgotten that. "Rose must be happy."

"I think this is great," Mom said. "All these exciting new developments—first Joy, then Max . . . Does anyone else have any surprises for us?"

"So when's all this happening?" Dad asked.

"Would you believe Monday?" Uncle Max said. "I called yesterday and got the ticket. It cost an arm and a leg on such short notice, but what're you going to do? I'm just figuring to bring one small suitcase, and I'll be back on the Friday afternoon, unless, of course, I don't like it or something comes up, or I don't feel well. I've heard about plenty people dropping dead down there. . . ."

"You're not going to drop dead down there," Dad said. "The way you're going, you'll outlast all of us."

"You all look so thrilled that I'm leaving. You're not going to give my room away?" Uncle Max turned to Mom and then to me. "It's still going to be waiting for me when I get back, right?"

"What are you talking about?" Dad said. "Of course it will."

"You don't have to worry." Mom put her hand on his. "It's your room," she said.

Chapter 29

"I hate good-byes," said Uncle Max Monday morning. "I don't believe in them. What's more, this isn't one. So let's not have any fuss, all right?"

"No fuss," we all agreed. We were too nice to point out that he himself had fussed nonstop since Thanksgiving. So he gave us each a big hug and a kiss, we patted Sarge, and that was that.

"Well, I'm hoping he enjoys himself," Mom said that night. "Honestly, though? Set in his ways as he is . . ."

"It's not that likely," Dad finished for her. When Uncle Max called, he made his voice extra hearty. "So how is it down there in sunny Florida?" he asked.

"Sunny," said Uncle Max. We were all on the line. "The bread's god-awful, though. Spongy white bread, that's all you see. And the water tastes funny. Everyone drinks bottled water."

"Have you taken up golf yet?" Dad asked the next night.

"Golf?" said Uncle Max. "I'm doing the exact same things I do at home—sit in my chair, do the puzzle, play a little solitaire, some pinochle, get on people's nerves. . . . It's very hot. And you never saw such big cockroaches in your life. One came up out of the drain earlier. Sarge took one look and left the room."

"How's Rose?" Mom asked later that week.

"Rose is Rose," he said. "You know her. She's always got some plan or other. One day an art gallery, another, something at the library. Who knew she was such a culture vulture?"

"And you go with her?" I asked.

"So far I've managed to weasel out of it," he said.

"He's impossible!" Mom said when we got off. "I don't know if I'm hoping he's hanging out with Rose so he's not lonely, or that he keeps to himself, so that he doesn't immediately drive her up the wall. I mean, if even he says he's already getting on everybody's nerves . . ."

This was new, Mom saying something anti-Max. Dad and I looked at her. All sorts of new things were happening since Uncle Max had gone. We'd been out for dinner twice, both times to places Uncle Max would never eat. Dad was coming home a little earlier. Mom already looked less harried. The drop in bickering was dramatic. Though I couldn't tell if it was my improved home life making my spirits soar, or that I was so happy about Max.

We'd just come back from an Indian restaurant the next night when Uncle Max called. "How's the food there? Are you eating okay?" Mom asked.

He hmmphed into the phone. "I try telling Rose there's no need for her to cook me dinner every day, but you know her, she says, 'I'm cooking anyway.' She's a very good cook, but she talks a lot, Rose. She talks even more than Sy. If it were a little more interesting, I wouldn't mind so much. . . . I'm going to need a vacation from my vacation."

"Complains a lot, doesn't he?" Dad said afterward. Mom rolled her eyes.

"He hasn't left, though," I pointed out. "I think he's having a good time."

"I don't know about him," Mom said. "I'm having a great time! I forgot what a peaceful life we had pre-Max. I can put the spoons in the dishwasher any way I want. I can roll the socks inside out. I love him, but for a very small man, he sure took up a lot of room."

"Just remember," Dad said. "You said it, not me. And don't be too quick to put him in the past tense. He'll be back in a week."

"You're right," she said. "Let's enjoy it while it lasts."

The next night, for the first time, he didn't call. (I

didn't learn that till later, since a bunch of us had gone to Max's and we'd ordered pizza.) "I hope you weren't too worried about me," he said when he finally called Sunday afternoon. "I was out till very late, playing cards. Then today, we went for brunch. And tonight, they want me to go to the track, no less."

"The racetrack?" Nathan asked. We still always all got on when he called.

"Yeah. You think I should go with them? I might lose my shirt. Oh, and by the way, I shipped us a big box of grapefruits," he said. "They should be arriving any day. They're excellent, but don't eat them all. Make sure you save some for me."

I was right. He *was* having a good time.

"Good time is overstating it," he said when I suggested that. "It's okay, except that I'm so far away. I don't know what you're up to anymore. I ask you how you are, you say fine. I ask what's new, you say nothing much."

"We're just doing the same stuff," Dad said. "You're not missing anything exciting."

"You I don't expect excitement from," he said. "But Nathan and Joy . . . I miss being right there. Nathan, how's the math coming? Joy, how's your love life? How's Young Max?"

"Max is good," I said.

"Just good? That's all you're going to say?"

"Very good," I said.

"So have you gotten a look at him yet, Ilene? Has he been over?"

"He was here yesterday, in fact," Mom said. "He seems very nice."

"See what I mean?" he said. "I'm missing everything. I'm glad you approve of him, though. He's a class act. And Mabel, Joy? How's Mabel?"

"She's not Mabel anymore," I said. "She's Mint."

"Mint?" He chuckled. "First she's a tree, now she's a tea. Was she over, too? Are you two still in business?"

"She's mostly in the music business," I said, "so I doubt she'll be over much, but we're friends. I'm riding to school with her every day again." This was one of the bonuses of my new thing with Max. I didn't have to leave so ridiculously early in the morning to get to see him.

"See, this is what I mean," he said. "I'm used to knowing all this. I've gotten spoiled being right there with you."

"I can write you a letter if you want," said Nathan.

"And when you get back, we'll fill you in on everything," Dad said.

"And you'll have a lot to tell us, too," I said.

There was a silence. "Actually," he said, "I'm trying to decide what I should do. Mimi's progressing, but the doctor thinks she shouldn't travel yet. Her condo's going to be available another week at least." He paused again. "What do you think?"

I thought Mom and Dad would drop their phones and dance a jig.

"It's up to you," Dad said.

"Completely," Mom said.

"You might need to send me down a few more things," he said.

"Should we also send down your Hanukkah presents?" she asked. Which was the wrong thing to say. I knew that instantly.

"Don't jump the gun, okay, Ilene?" he said. "It's not Hanukkah yet. I'll be back by then." But then he said, "Listen, I shouldn't stay on too long. I don't want to run up Rose's long distance."

The next week he didn't call quite as much. Instead we started getting postcards. The first one, addressed to Nathan, said he'd won eight dollars at the track. GREETINGS FROM PARROT JUNGLE! said the next. The one from the Serpentarium said *I didn't like crocodiles before I went here. I like them even less now.* We got postcards from an art museum, some flamingo garden, and one with a picture of a humongous crab, that said *I ate this guy for dinner.*

"So, Max, how're you getting to all these places?" Dad asked when he did call.

"Oh, didn't I mention it?" he said. "We rented a car."

We all looked at one another. "Don't ask," Mom told us.

"That 'don't ask' sounded just like Uncle Max," I said when we got off.

"You mean it's contagious?" she said, wrinkling her nose.

"I didn't mean that in a bad way," I said. "I actually sort of miss him." Which was true. I missed having him around when I got home from school. I missed Sarge greeting me at the door.

"I miss Max," Dad said. "Just not enough to want him to come rushing back. If you ask me, talking to him on the phone for a few minutes every day or two is the ideal arrangement—we know he's fine, but he has his own life."

"I'd feel so good," Mom said, "if he had his own life."

"I'd feel so good if I had my own room!" Nathan said.

For two weeks now, I'd restrained myself from saying that!

"We know," Dad said, "but it's not a good idea."

"It's the old umbrella principle," Mom said. "The minute we move Joy's stuff out of your room, Mrs.

Posner will have a miraculous recovery and he'll be on the next plane."

"What's up with Mrs. Posner, anyway?" Dad said. "How's she doing? Nobody's said a word in over a week. We need to plan. We should ask."

"I don't know about that," Mom said. "I'd vote for letting sleeping dogs lie."

Her sarcasm still always took me by surprise. The whole three months he'd been here, she'd been earnestness personified. Come to think of it, she was pretty earnest before he got here, too. A mom with an edge would sure liven things up when he got back. Which led me to a weird and interesting thought. Were things so much better now because Uncle Max was gone, or because he'd been here?

I didn't move any of my things, but that week I began sleeping in my old room again. It didn't bother me that it smelled like old dog and old man. It had a door and no Nathan; that's all that counted.

"Have you noticed that he's not mentioning the Karetskys lately, only Rose?" Mom asked somewhere in here. "D'you think they've had a falling out?"

"The other possibility being . . ." Dad's smile was impish. "I mean, for all we know . . ."

"Max and Rose?" Mom shook her head. "No. Not possible." She shook her head again. "It's too outlandish."

"What's outlandish?" asked Nathan.

Mom raised her eyebrows. "Your father thinks Uncle Max and Mrs. Nussbaum might be romantically involved."

"*Eeeooh!*" Nathan wrinkled his nose.

"You're eleven, Nathan," I said. "You know nothing."

"That may well be," said Dad, "but the mind does sort of boggle."

Mine didn't, but I didn't say anything.

As we got farther into December, both the cards and phone calls dwindled. It was the second day of Hanukkah when his check arrived with a short note. *Sorry this is so late,* it said. *Have some fun with it. Marty, how about getting yourself some new art supplies?*

What we bought, though, was ice skates. I thought we were just buying skates for me. Jen loved skating, and it turned out Max did, too, so I'd been going to the rink in Central Park with them and renting. But when we got to the store, Mom decided we all needed skates. She got so psyched about it that when winter vacation started, she wanted to go skating every day. Dad and Nathan were a hard sell, so a few times, when I wasn't doing things with Max and my friends, I went with her. It was actually somewhat fun. We'd just come back from skating when the letter came.

273 ★

"Maybe there's another check inside," Nathan said as Mom ripped it open.

Mom gave him a look. "I hope it's not bad news," she said. *"Dear All,"* she started reading. *"I never could understand why Rose raved so much about Florida . . .* Oh, Lord!" She looked up at Dad.

"The honeymoon's over?" Dad said.

She frowned. "That's what it sounds like."

"What does he say?" I said.

"He says, *Florida's fine if you like spongy bagels and don't mind spending all your time with a bunch of Golden Agers, but even with the slush, I'll take Manhattan. Rose, however, is a new woman down here. She looks ten years younger. She claims it's the company. . . ."* Mom looked up. "See what I mean?"

"No," I said, "keep reading."

"She claims it's the company, but if you ask me, it's because the condo has no sad reminders of her past life. And you should see Sarge. He's like a new dog here. The lampshade, as Joy calls it, has been off for a week now. No more scratching! Between the two of them, they're running me ragged. The upshot of all this, since Mimi Posner isn't doing as well as anyone expected, seems to be that Sarge and I will stick around here for a while. That will also give me more time to get used to what I am about to tell you.

You'll probably think I'm crazy. It's always hard to know when you're doing something for yourself and when you're doing it for someone else. When you took me in, there was no question that it was for my sake more than yours. In this case, it's much more complicated. On the other hand, as my good friend Sy Karetsky tells me every time I try to discuss it with him: What's the difference why you're doing it, it's the best idea you've had since Nathan's Shoes. I evidently think he's right.

Anyway, I'm thinking that in the spring, assuming we all last that long, Rose should have a real fresh start, not just a winter break. It has also been pointed out by all and sundry that a fresh start wouldn't be the worst thing in the world for me either. You might wonder just how much freshness (not to mention how much of a start) is feasible for an old fossil. I'm wondering the same thing. As they say down here in Codger Country, at our age, you don't even buy green bananas! But enough beating around the bush. I hope this doesn't come as a complete shock. Rose and I have decided to move into your apartment."

"What?" Dad practically erupted. "Both of them? No. Forget it! I'll kill myself. I swear to God, I'll jump right out the window!"

Mom looked down the page. "Oh, my God!" she

said. "Come look at this!" From her face, I couldn't tell if it was very good or really bad. We all crowded around and read over her shoulder.

"*I've loved being with you, just not right on top of you. And I expect, though you are far too kind and generous to ever say so, that the feeling's mutual. So the plan is we'll do a swap. Ingenious, eh? You folks will move to my apartment. Rose will dispose of her place, which, though it is full of happy memories as well as sad, is way too big to take care of. Her nephew, Jay, who is in real estate, says she should get a pretty penny for it. She also spoke to her cousin's daughter, a lawyer and a very smart cookie, who will be calling you in a few days about the financial end.*

I can hear you already, Ilene, worrying about the money. Don't. It's about time you all had enough room to spread out. We could wait for all this to happen until I die, but what fun is that for me? I'd like to see Ilene with a proper office to do her schoolwork, and Marty will be a lot happier with his own studio so he can paint again, which I happen to know he misses even though he never talks about it. The walls in my building are thick enough so Nathan can play his electric guitar without giving everyone a headache, and Joy can stop doing her homework in a closet. She isn't a kid anymore, Ilene. She's a young woman. She needs her own room. So does Nathan, of course, but for Joy it is crucial. (Joy, I'm sure, will not have failed to note that the apartment is six blocks closer to Young Max's.) The place will require some fixing up, but that shouldn't present a problem. Rose has a cousin in the remodeling business. Will call to discuss.

> *Your loving uncle,*
> *Maxwell Mitnick*

P.S. Rose dragged me to a lecture the other day. I fell asleep, but she didn't notice. Now she's hot to get me on one of those giant tricycles. I told her fat chance, but stranger things have already happened. . . .

P.P.S. So what does all this mean? For you, it should be pretty good. For me, I'll let you know when I find out.

P.P.P.S. Joy, my sweet girl, you are allowed to gloat!"